# Dog Knows

## A golden retriever mystery

### Neil S. Plakcy

**Reviews for the series:**

Mr. Plakcy did a terrific job in this cozy mystery. He had a smooth writing style that kept the story flowing evenly. The dialogue and descriptions were right on target. --Red Adept

Steve and Rochester become quite a team and Neil Plakcy is the kind of writer that I want to tell me this story. It's a fun read which will keep you turning pages very quickly. Amos Lassen – Amazon top 100 reviewer

In Dog We Trust is a very well-crafted mystery that kept me guessing up until Steve figured out where things were going. --E-book addict reviews

Neil Plakcy's Kingdom of Dog is supposed to be about the former computer hacker, now college professor, Steve Levitan, but it is his golden retriever Rochester who is the real amateur sleuth in this delightful academic mystery. This is no talking dog book, though. Rochester doesn't need anything more than his wagging tail and doggy smile to win over readers and help solve crimes. I absolutely fell in love with this brilliant dog who digs up clues and points the silly humans towards the evidence. – Christine Kling, author of *Circle of Bones*

This book is for Brody and Griffin, and for their daddy.

A big sloppy golden thank you to Christine Jackson, Sharon Potts and Ramona DeFelice Long, for their help in bringing this book together.

# Contents

# 1 – The Girl She Was

Rochester clambered up onto the sofa next to me and rested his head on my lap, as if he was sharing the weight of the world with me. I stroked his golden flanks and told him what a good puppy he was, and he snuffled against my hand.

My golden retriever was five years old, though we didn't know his exact age or birthday because he'd been a rescue. In his way, he'd rescued me, too, because I was in a bad place when he came into my life. Looking back, he was only one of those who'd stepped in when I needed someone — the most recent, of course, being my girlfriend Lili, who came toward the sofa and surveyed the situation.

"Not much room for me, is there?" she said, her hands on her hips.

"We'll always make room for you." I shifted a few inches toward the arm of the sofa, and reorganized Rochester's eighty-pound bulk so Lili could join us. She was a shapely woman, though not quite what my father would have called zaftig. Just enough curves to satisfy me, auburn hair in a loose curl, and a smiling mouth perfect for kissing.

Which was what I did as soon as she was settled. I was a couple of inches taller than she was, but sitting together like that our height difference didn't matter. Rochester sat up in the space between us, staring at us as we kissed, and I had to pull away and rub under his chin. "Nobody's ignoring you, puppy," I said. "But sometimes Mama Lili and I need some us time."

She scratched under his belly, and he opened his mouth wide in a big doggy grin. We were chilling like that when my phone rang with a call from Hunter Thirkell, an attorney in the small Bucks County town of Stewart's Crossing where we lived. I was surprised because it was eight o'clock at night.

I'd met Hunter a few years before, when he handled my father's estate. He had a brash, New York personality at odds with our sleepy Pennsylvania town, but he'd created a thriving practice in everything from wills and power of attorney to criminal defense, and he'd represented me years before when I had to meet with the police as I investigated the murder of my next-door neighbor.

"Hey, Steve, how's the hacking game going?" he asked. His voice was so loud that Rochester perked up his ears. Lili got up and went over to the dining room table, where she opened her laptop.

Hunter knew that I'd served a year in the California prison system for computer hacking, and whenever I ran into him around town, he'd tease me about the latest hacking case and ask if I was involved.

I didn't appreciate being reminded of the past I'd worked so hard to put behind me, and even though I understood that was his awkward way of maintaining a friendship, vague as it was, I did my best to shut down any questions.

"Listen, Hunter. I don't do that stuff anymore, and I'm tired of you bringing it up."

I was about to hang up when he said, "Steve, wait. I'm sorry. I know I go overboard sometimes."

"You do."

"But I need your help, and I don't know anyone else I can ask."

"My help with what?"

"I took on a new client. Maybe you've heard about her in the news. The Black Widow of Birch Valley."

"I've heard of her," I said. "Margaret something, right? Aren't they saying she killed three husbands in a row?"

"That's what the press is pushing. But right now she's just accused of killing the last one, a bum who died when the brakes failed on his motorcycle."

"And this has what to do with me?"

"She insists that the bum had a lot of bad shit going on, that he was always emailing people, though she never saw any of the messages. We know from the evidence the police collected that right before he died, he wiped out everything in his email account. She's sure that if somebody can retrieve all that stuff, it will exonerate her. The police have his laptop but they're not doing shit to recover anything from it. I need somebody who can go into his email account and get back everything he deleted."

"There are companies that can do that," I said.

Rochester sniffed at the hand holding the phone, and I scratched him behind his ears with my other hand.

"And they'll charge through the nose," Hunter said. "I took this case pro bono because I believe Peggy's innocent."

"Peggy? I thought her name was Margaret."

"Yeah, that's her legal name. But I used to see her dance at Club Hott, back when I was going through my divorce, and she went by Peggy then."

"Come on, Hunter. You're lusting after an exotic dancer who's already killed three husbands?"

Rochester butted his head against my leg. I didn't know what he was trying to tell me—should I be nicer to Hunter? Get him off the phone? I gently pushed him away.

"I'm not lusting after her, Steve. She's a good lady who's had a rough life."

"She told you that while she was giving you a lap dance?"

"You know what? Forget I asked. I'll find somebody else. Somebody with a shred of human decency."

He must have been on a land line, because I heard a bang through the phone as he hung up. This time, when Rochester put his paws up on my leg and leveraged himself up to face me, I scratched under his chin. "Don't worry, puppy, I'm not going to get in trouble."

Lili looked up from the dining room table. "I don't normally like to pry in your conversations but that one just begs for explanation."

"Hunter Thirkell." Lili had met him once or twice when we were out and about in Stewart's Crossing. "He's representing that woman accused of killing three husbands."

"I read an article about her in the *Boat-Gazette*," Lili said. That was the local paper for Stewart's Crossing, a mix of local ads and digested versions of Bucks County and national news. "She met her first husband when they were students at the community college. He overdosed a couple of years into their marriage."

"He was a junkie?"

"Apparently his parents died when he was a kid, leaving all their assets in a trust fund for him. He started using to medicate his pain, and eventually it got to be too much for him."

"And her second husband?"

"He was a drug dealer, and he forced Margaret to be his mule, bringing drugs in from South America. She got caught, flipped on him, and then he died before he could go to trial."

"Ouch. Two bad husbands in a row."

"Tell me about it. Though at least neither of mine were into drugs the way hers were."

She sighed. "I kind of empathized with her because I've been through two husbands myself, though I never had any interest in killing either of them."

"Good to know. Hunter says the third husband was a biker who died when his brakes failed. That tally with what you read?"

She nodded. "The article said she had means, motive and opportunity in all three deaths. What does Hunter want from you?"

"To retrieve the last victim's emails, because he thinks they'll exonerate his client."

"And the lap dance part?"

"She was an exotic dancer at Club Hott in Levittown for a while," I said. "That's how Hunter made her acquaintance."

"I remember that from the article," Lili said. "That's

how she met husband number three."

Rochester jumped to the floor and rolled on his back. He waved his legs in the air—his equivalent of an exotic dance, letting me know he wanted his belly rubbed. I got down on the floor beside him and obeyed.

"Hunter gets around," Lili said.

"That he does."

"You going to help him?"

I shook my head. "I don't want to put myself in jeopardy to help a total stranger, who's most likely killed three times. Let the criminal justice system work."

Despite the fact that I'd gone to prison myself, I had faith in the system. I did the crime, and did the time. Everyone I met while I was incarcerated was guilty of something, even if it wasn't the specific crime he'd been sentenced for. Sure, I'd read of cases where poor, illiterate people of color had been railroaded for crimes they didn't commit, but that didn't seem the case here.

Lili went back to her grading, and I played with Rochester on the floor for a couple of minutes. But Hunter's plea kept echoing in my head, and I couldn't resist the urge to see what the papers were saying about his client. To paraphrase a quote I'd heard somewhere, losing one husband was unfortunate, two careless, and three downright criminal.

I sat across from Lili at the dining room table and opened my laptop. I was intrigued at the tabloid-like story that spilled forth from newspaper websites. Margaret Landsea had married a kid she met in her political science class, whose parents had died in a car crash when he was twelve. The insurance settlement had gone into a seven-figure trust fund for him, which he was able to access when he turned twenty-one.

With all that money, you'd think the couple would have been set for life, but according to the article the young man suffered the loss of his parents greatly, and he soothed that pain with illicit drugs. Three years into his marriage to Peggy, he died of a heroin overdose.

At the time, no one questioned the situation. He was a junkie without any family beyond his wife, who had been hustled into a rehab program. Eventually she remarried, a Colombian who went by the name of Juan Perez—though eventual investigation revealed that was about as false as every other thing in his life. Nine years into that marriage, she was arrested as she arrived in Miami on a flight from Medellin. The customs agent noticed she was sweating profusely, and upon examination she was discovered to be carrying six condoms filled with cocaine in her vagina.

She avoided jail time by turning state's evidence

against Perez. Before he could go to trial, though, he was found dead in their home. The coroner believed that he had been attempting to inject heroin into his veins, but accidentally introduced a bubble of air instead, causing a fatal heart attack.

After another stint in rehab, Margaret began dancing at Club Hott. I did a quick records search and found that Hunter's divorce had gone through a few months after Perez's death. So it made sense that he'd have run into her then, some seven years before.

Hunter had remarried a couple of years later, and according to the newspaper Margaret Perez had met and married husband number three, Carl Landsea, about the same time. He was a shift supervisor at US Steel's Fairless Plant, and an active member of a biker group called Levitt's Angels.

After four years of marriage, he died in a motorcycle accident, and an investigation revealed that someone had tampered with his brakes. Within a few weeks after Carl's death, Margaret Landsea had been arrested, based on evidence provided by an anonymous caller and later verified by Margaret herself that Carl was abusive toward her.

That's when the story hit the news, and I realized I'd been following it off and on for the past three months. An eager young district attorney had discovered the deaths of her previous two husbands, and a reporter for the Bucks County *Courier Times* had coined the "Black Widow of Birch Valley" nickname, after the Levittown neighborhood where she and Carl had lived.

The reporter had assembled a collage of photos of Peggy at different times. In a fuzzy group shot, she was a freckle-faced teen posing with the pre-law club. In her mug shot from the drug mule arrest, she looked old before her time, with bags under her eyes, her hair a scary mess of tangles like Medusa. A promotional photo from her Club Hott days focused more on her figure, with a narrow waist and artificially enlarged breasts, but when I zoomed in on her face I saw the same sadness.

She looked familiar, and I knew she was about my age—had I known her at some point?

I looked at Rochester, who was snoozing on the floor. No help there.

I went back to the article. Her name was Margaret Ann Doyle Stanwood Perez Landsea. Hunter had called her Peggy, though.

Peggy Doyle. "Oh, shit," I said out loud.

Lili looked up. "What?"

"I know her," I said. "At least I did when I was a kid. Peggy Doyle."

"She went to school with you?"

I nodded. "More than that. I told you my parents sent me on a summer study program to France when I was a teenager, didn't I?"

She nodded. "You said you were too young but they sent you anyway."

"I was a couple of months short of my fifteenth birthday, and everybody else on the course was older. But I was shy, always had my nose in a book, and my parents thought that sending me on a summer study program abroad would open up my horizons and give me more self-confidence."

Our school system was a wealthy one, full of the sons and daughters of doctors, lawyers and engineers, and the administration was keen on offering lots of opportunities for us. I could have studied Spanish in Salamanca, German in Frankfurt, or European history in Luxembourg. Instead my parents chose the French language program at the University of Grenoble.

"I didn't know any of the other kids, but Peggy adopted me and I tagged along with her and her friends. I never would have taken the cable car up to look over Grenoble, gone to the beach in Nice, or found my way to the Sainte-Chapelle in Paris, if she hadn't taken me under her wing."

Lili smiled. "You were such a cutie pie back then. I've seen the pictures. So skinny you disappeared if you turned sideways, with that mop of brown hair."

"And I'm not a cutie pie now?" I protested.

"You filled out, and you're losing your hair. Today I'd call you handsome, not cute."

I was mollified. "Peggy was so full of energy and enthusiasm that I couldn't help liking her. Gradually I learned her back story – she was the oldest of four girls born in rat-a-tat order. She grew up in a run-down neighborhood in Trenton. Her father was a drunk who rarely worked, and her mother was a maid. Her father died when she was nine, and Peggy had to take care of her younger sisters and at night, help her mother with ironing and dressmaking."

"That's so sad," Lili said. "How did she get to Stewart's Crossing?"

Sad was one of Rochester's words—whenever he heard someone say it, he hopped up and offered comfort in the form of a cold black nose and a long pink tongue. Lili petted him as he rested his head in her lap.

"Three years after her father died, her mother married a widower she'd been cleaning for and moved the girls here to one of the big split levels on the other side of town. Once her family had some money, she babysat for neighbors, walked dogs and did whatever she could so she could go on that trip to France. I was amazed that after everything she'd been through, she was so eager to reach out and grasp everything the world had to offer."

"I'd think the opposite," Lili said. "That her background would make her eager to see what the rest of the world was like."

I shook my head. "That's because of who you are, and the way your parents moved around so much when you were a kid. Lots of the kids I grew up with had no desire to leave Bucks County—they wouldn't even go on field trips to New York or Philadelphia. Look at Rick – he's never lived anywhere but here."

Rick Stemper was my best friend, a police detective in Stewart's Crossing. He had gone to the community college and the affiliated police academy, and he was perfectly happy to spend the rest of his life in his hometown.

"It doesn't sound like Peggy got far, either" Lili said.

"She tried, at least. When we got home from France, she was a senior and I was a sophomore, and we stayed friendly. Her stepfather bought an old car for her so she could shepherd her sisters around to gymnastics and dance class, but every now and then she'd pick me up and we'd go to a jazz concert at the high school, or we'd take the train into Philadelphia and go to the Museum of Art. Once we even ran up the stairs like Rocky. Peggy waved her arms in the air as if she'd won the lottery."

"Sounds like she was very lucky."

"Peggy always said that she was. The summer after our trip to France, she was baby-sitting for a family who lived about a mile from my house, and once a week or so I'd walk over there so we could hang out."

I remembered those long walks from one suburban neighborhood to the next. There were no gated communities then, and one street flowed into another. Many moms stayed at home, driveways were filled with station wagons and riding toys, sprinklers went off and the streets were filled with the sounds of kids romping in backyard pools.

"The kids Peggy was taking care of were pretty young and easily occupied with building blocks and Barbies, and we'd sit out on the screened-in patio and talk about our futures," I said to Lili. "Peggy was determined to be an attorney and advocate for kids. She'd known many broken families back in Trenton, and seen how few opportunities were available to the kids. She knew how incredibly lucky she and her sisters were, that their stepfather had brought them out of the city slums to the safety and comfort of the suburbs."

"Sounds like you guys spent a lot of time together," Lili said.

"I'm sure it wasn't all that much. My parents made me go to summer school in the mornings, and I had other friends to hang out with, too. But Peggy was different, maybe because she was older, or maybe because she was more goal-directed than my other friends. She got a small scholarship to Penn State but it wasn't enough to cover all her expenses and she decided to stay home and go to the community college for two years."

"That's not necessarily a bad thing," Lili said. "I know a lot of people who've gotten their early college work done in places like that."

"I know. And her ambition affected me, too. When I was in twelfth grade, she picked me up two nights a week and we drove up to Newtown, where we took introduction to psychology and freshman composition together."

I leaned forward and put my elbows on the dining room table. "I lost track of her after I went to Eastern, but I always assumed she'd gone on to law school as she planned and become a successful attorney."

"That didn't happen."

"I need to call Hunter back," I said. "If there's a chance that Peggy is innocent, and I can find something in her husband's emails to prove that, I ought to help her out. She was kind to me when I needed it, and I owe it to her to do the same thing."

Rochester turned his attention from Lili to me, and rested his big golden head on my knee, dripping a bit of saliva on my bare leg.

"Just be careful, Steve. Even if she's innocent, she's lost three husbands, been through drug problems and done a lot of things she probably isn't proud of. She may not even want your help, because you'll remind her of who she used to be."

"I'll be careful," I said. "But people believed in me when I was in trouble, and if there's a shred of the old Peggy left inside her, I want to help her bring it out."

# 2 – Slippery Slope

I called Hunter back, explained what I'd discovered, and made an appointment to meet at his office early the next morning, on my way to work. While Lili continued to grade papers, I reread the information I'd found online. I didn't want the Peggy Doyle I'd known as a kid to be guilty of murder. If she was innocent of killing husband number three, I didn't want her to have to relive the pain of the deaths of her first two husbands, and I certainly didn't want her to go to jail.

Memories came back to me. Peggy vamping in front of an expensive jewelry store in Paris, then egging a group of us to climb the 387 steps to the top of Notre Dame cathedral. Peggy and me, riding up to those night classes. She had worked all day at a dry cleaner's, but she still had so much energy.

Too bad the classes we took hadn't been up to par. Sure, they'd been a bit tougher than high school, but unfortunately they gave me a false impression of college. When I applied to get credit at Eastern for the psych course I discovered that what we took a whole term to study, the class at Eastern handled in the first eight weeks.

I turned to Lili and told her that. "And when I submitted the syllabus for the freshman comp course, I got turned down for that, too—I hadn't written enough papers or used enough sources to qualify."

"I'm surprised Eastern was so picky back then," Lili said. "Nowadays when I get a request for transfer credit for a course I almost always rubber-stamp it. Of course it's different in arts classes."

I still taught a class in the English department each term, to keep my hand in and because I genuinely liked teaching, and Lili and I often compared notes on how poorly prepared some of our students were.

"Yeah, well, times were different back then, I guess. My dad was pretty pissed—he thought he was going to save some money on my tuition because I was coming in with credits. He and my Mom made too much money together for me to qualify for most of the government financial aid – it was a couple of years before they loosened up the requirements for middle-income families. For the rest of my four years he grumbled about it, even though I got some scholarships and a work-study grant that made up for it anyway."

"Don't get me started on parents and the cost of college," Lili said. "My father went ballistic when I dropped out to marry Adriano. After he and I divorced and I went back to school for photography, my father insisted that studying how to take pictures was only one step up from basket-weaving."

"Did any college ever offer classes in that?" I asked. "Because that was one of my father's tics, too."

"I'm sure some college did."

Rochester started whimpering and sniffing and I realized it was time for his last walk before bed. It was a hot night, with heat lightning streaking the sky, and I felt unsettled, despite my dog's comforting presence.

I slept restlessly, weird dreams about Peggy and France and women's prisons. It was a relief when Rochester woke me as soon as the sun was up for his morning walk. While he danced around my feet, and Lili buried her head in the pillow, I pulled on my regular dog walk attire: a tank top, shorts and sneakers.

Rochester was a very inquisitive dog, and he often tugged me forward in search of new and exciting smells. Every now and then I'd have to assert control, though. "No, Rochester. We're not going backwards. Come on, you've sniffed that enough. If you're not going to pee on it then keep moving."

My neighbor Bob Freehl was on his knees in his driveway, weeding the floral border alongside it. He was a retired Stewart's Crossing cop, with a burly build and thinning gray hair. "You talk to that dog like he understands you," he said.

"He does," I said. "Hey, Bob, you know anything about the Black Widow of Birch Valley case?"

"Just what I read in the papers. She's got to be guilty as sin."

"You can't know that," I said.

"I spent enough time on the force to get a nose for this kind of thing," he said. "Exotic dancer, drug addict. If she didn't do it herself, she got someone to do it for her."

"I hope they don't put you on her jury," I said.

"No worry about that. Soon as a defense attorney finds out I was a cop, I get excused. Happened three times so far. You'd think they'd just put something in their system and not bother me. You ever get called for jury duty?"

"Once, when I was living in California." I neglected to mention that I'd also been on the other side of the courtroom, as the defendant in a criminal case – the hacking one Hunter was so eager to remind me of.

My wife at the time had suffered a miscarriage and comforted herself with extreme retail therapy, putting us deeply in debt. I'd worked overtime and freelance gigs to pay off those bills, and when she got pregnant again I thought all was right in the world.

When she miscarried a second time, I was determined

not to repeat the mistakes of the past, so I hacked into the three major credit bureaus and put flags on her accounts. I did it because I could, because I had an outsized level of hubris about my computer skills and because it seemed easier than confronting the real problem with her.

I got caught, of course, and served my time. Spent endless hours in group meetings to control my addiction to hacking, joined an online support group. But somewhere in the back of my mind I hadn't quite reformed, though I had promised Lili and Rick that I would only snoop into places online that wouldn't get me sent back to prison. I guess Rochester and I were a good match, both of us very nosey.

Rochester pulled forward, and I said goodbye to Bob and tried to focus on the present, on the blessings of my life instead of on my past. I had adopted Rochester after the death of his previous owner, my next-door neighbor, and his unconditional love had gone a long way toward healing me.

By the time we returned to the house, I was drenched in sweat and Rochester was panting madly. I gave him a few minutes to cool down, then poured some kibble into his bowl. He looked up at me with a mournful expression. "I know, same shit, different day," I said. "That's all you're getting so you might as well enjoy it."

If dogs could shrug, then that's what he did. He stuck

his big snout into the bowl and started scarfing up the pellets. While he ate I showered and dressed, thinking about my meeting with Hunter that morning. Since Rochester went to work with me every day, he'd either come into the office with Hunter or wait outside for me.

We navigated the back roads outside Stewart's Crossing to Hunter's office, in a co-working space out by the highway. From the parking lot I called him. "I have my dog with me. Okay if I bring him in?"

"Sure, we have dogs in here all the time," he said, so I hooked up Rochester's leash and kept him on a tight rein as we walked into the lobby, where a receptionist directed us down the hall to Hunter's office. We passed several empty conference rooms, and a big open space where a couple of young guys sat with coffee, talking.

When I first met Hunter, he was a portly guy, but he seemed to have expanded greatly since then. The buttons on his shirt threatened to pop as he lounged back in his chair. He was about five years younger than I was, but all that weight made him seem older. We shook hands, and he petted Rochester, and then I sat across from his desk, with Rochester collapsed on the floor beside me.

"What do you know about Peggy?" Hunter asked.

I went through how Peggy and I met on the trip to

France, became friends, then lost touch. "I know a lot about her childhood, but anything after I left for college I only know from what I read in the papers."

"And they only print what they think will get a rise out of people," Hunter said. "I'm glad you knew her back then, because you won't believe all the bad stuff."

"People change," I said. "I sure have since the last time I saw Peggy. But I'm keeping an open mind. What can you tell me that I wouldn't have read in the papers?"

"Let's start with her first husband, the trustafarian."

"He was a Rastafarian?" I'd seen a photo of him and he didn't look black, or have dreadlocks.

Hunter laughed. "No, it's a slang term for a kid who lives off a family trust fund. Bobby Stanwood was a sad case, from all I've heard. His parents were killed in a car crash when he was about twelve, and the resulting lawsuit left him with a big trust fund. But no amount of money matters when you suffer a loss that big, and despite his aunt and uncle taking him in and caring for him, he started medicating his pain with illicit drugs as soon as he could get access to them."

I nodded. I'd seen some of that in my fellow prisoners in California.

"He and Peggy had a good time for a couple of years. She struggled to keep him going in college, but eventually he was mainlining heroin on a regular basis. Two years into their marriage he overdosed. No suspicion of Peggy at the time. She inherited what was left of his trust fund, but she had a habit of her own by then, and she ran through it quickly. She's a smart gal, too smart for her own good sometimes, and she hid her habit from everybody who cared about her."

Too smart for her own good. The same phrase had been applied to me when I was in prison, and again by my parole officer. Another thing Peggy and I had in common.

Rochester stood up and nuzzled my leg, and I petted him as Hunter continued with Peggy's story.

"She needed more and more money for her habit, so she started trading sex for drugs, and eventually she got arrested about two years after Bobby died. Charges were dropped on condition that she enter a detox program, and she did. She moved back home with her mom — the step-dad had died by that point."

I realized that about that time, I had gotten my MA in English from Columbia and begun dating Mary, the woman I'd marry soon after. How different our lives had been at that point.

"She got a secretarial job, and then entered a part-time course to become certified as a legal secretary," Hunter continued. "But then her mom got sick, and Peggy dropped out to take care of her. Despite all the pain pills her mom had, Peggy stayed clean."

"Was she in Narcotics Anonymous or one of those other twelve-step programs?" I asked. "Because I find that hard to believe. People with addictive personalities go back to whatever helps them when things get tough."

"That's what she told me, and I believe her," Hunter said. "And when her mother died a year and a half later, she went back to school and got her certificate as a legal secretary. She couldn't have done that if she was hooked on pills."

Was Hunter naïve? Or just determined to believe the best of his client? I didn't challenge him on it, though, because Rochester distracted me by walking around the chair where I sat, then slumping to the floor halfway between me and Hunter.

"With her credentials, Peggy eventually got a job as a legal secretary for a jerk in Levittown," Hunter continued.

"I assume you know the jerk."

"Only professionally, if you can call him a professional. An ambulance chaser with the morals of a snake. He forgot to file some paperwork on a case, but blamed her for it when he lost. He kicked Peggy to the curb and refused to give her a reference."

He shook his head. "By this time she was in her late

thirties and she couldn't cope anymore. That's when she went back to drugs, met this loser Colombian guy who went by the name Juan Perez. Though eventually it turns out that was just one of many aliases."

"That's the guy who married her and turned her into a drug mule?" I asked.

Rochester stood up again, and moved restlessly around Hunter's small office, sniffing at the law books on the shelves behind me.

"Yeah, a real prince among men," Hunter said. "Peggy pled down to a felony in exchange for testimony against him, but he died before he could go to trial."

"Was there any suspicion then that Peggy was involved in his death?"

"Apparently the DA at the time had a lot of questions for her about how Perez got his fixes, did Peggy ever help him, that kind of thing. Eventually, though, the coroner ruled it death by misadventure, which means that she attributed the death to an accident that occurred due to a dangerous risk that was taken voluntarily."

"So Peggy's a widow for the second time," I said. "How did she end up at Club Hott?"

"There aren't many options available to a pretty woman with a felony conviction and a spotty work record,"

Hunter said, and I resisted the urge to interrupt with possible choices. "She started stripping, trying to make some money and turn her life around."

"That's where you come in."

Rochester had moved over to a pile of papers on a low credenza beside the door, but I was too interested in what Hunter was saying to worry about reining him in.

"I won't apologize for hanging out at a titty bar," Hunter said. "I was divorced and lonely and Peggy and I clicked. Just a professional relationship, though. I found out she had been a legal secretary and I tried to get her a job. But nobody was willing to take a chance on her, and I've had the same gal since I opened this office so I couldn't take her on myself."

It was a shame. I'd been very lucky that people had taken a chance on me when I returned to Stewart's Crossing from my stint in prison.

"Around the same time I was trying to help her, she met Carl Landsea at the club, and he promised her the moon and stars if she'd marry him," Hunter said. "What choice did she have?"

"Did you know him?"

Hunter shrugged. "As much as you know any of the other regulars. I could tell he was an asshole, and I tried to steer Peggy away from him, but she shut me down. Then one day she wasn't there anymore, and one of the other girls told me she'd run off to Vegas with Landsea. That was the last I heard of her until she hit the news."

Rochester suddenly put his paws up on the credenza and started knocking papers around. "Rochester!" I said. "Stop that!"

A manila folder fell to the floor and popped open, and Rochester began sniffing it. "I'm sorry, Hunter," I said. "He's usually better behaved than this."

Rochester looked up at me with one of his doggy grins, then settled down beside me. I picked up the folder, which contained website printouts about a local motorcycle club called Levitt's Angels. Hunter had highlighted Carl Landsea's name on the first page.

I closed the folder but left it on my lap, and turned back to Hunter. "Did she contact you to represent her?"

He shook his head. "She had a court-appointed public defender, a kid with less than a year under his belt. He was encouraging her to take a plea deal that would have sent her to prison for a decade until I read about the case in the paper and intervened."

"You think she's innocent." It wasn't a question.

"I do. Landsea was lower than pond scum, and he must

have known something was going wrong or he wouldn't have erased all his emails just before he died."

"Unless Peggy erased them herself, after she killed him."

"Whose side are you on, Steve?"

"I'm on my own side, Hunter. I knew Peggy twenty years ago and she was a good kid, but she's had a lot of bad stuff go down since then. I know what that can do to you. So I'm not ready to blindly say she's innocent." I took a deep breath. "But I am willing to do what I can to help her out. You have the email account and password information?"

Hunter shook his head. "Can't you figure stuff like that out?" I could see the desperation in his face.

"I'd have to talk to Peggy," I said. "Most of the time, people use passwords they create from things in their background, like birthdays and phone numbers. Peggy could give me a lot of that information."

"Peggy is Carl's heir, and she has the authority to let you see anything he left behind. But you'll have to be very careful. If you find anything I need to be able to use it for her defense."

While Hunter picked up his phone to call Peggy, I sat back and thought about what I was getting myself into. Peggy Landsea could be nothing like the girl I remembered, and I knew well that I had the same kind of addictive personality – I had to be sure I didn't launch myself down a slippery slope into illegal activity on behalf of someone I didn't even recognize.

Rochester sniffed my hand, then licked it. I had a lot to lose if things went wrong. My job, my relationship with Lili, my freedom. My dog.

But something told me I had to see this through. I had to help Peggy the way she, and so many others, had helped me.

# 3 – Choosing Partners

Hunter turned away from me so that I couldn't hear his conversation. When he ended the call he looked back at me. "She remembers you. But she's embarrassed at the way her life has turned out and doesn't want your help."

"That's ridiculous. Tell me where I can find her. I'll convince her."

"I don't know, Steve. She's a pretty determined gal. And after all she's been through, I don't want to push her too much."

"Hunter. You need my help. Peggy needs my help. At least let me give it a try."

He blew a big breath out through pursed lips. "Fine. I'll write down her address for you, but I can't guarantee she'll answer the door. She was able to make bail by putting up her interest in Landsea's house in Birch Valley, and she has an ankle monitor to make sure she stays put."

While he wrote, I opened the Levitt's Angels folder on my lap. I figured the name was a play on words—a combination of Hell's Angels and William Levitt. He was the real estate developer who had built Levittown in the 1950s to house returning war vets and employees at the Fairless Works, at the time the largest open-pit steel mill in the country.

"Can I get a copy of this material?" I asked. "There might be some clues in it that would help me figure out Landsea's password."

"Take it. I have all the stuff bookmarked online. You'll see, Landsea was a real loser. If you can get into his email account and retrieve the messages he deleted, I'm sure there's going to be a message or a reference to some kind of crime that will point a finger at another suspect and raise some reasonable doubt that Peggy had anything to do with his death."

I took the address he had for Peggy, on Bark Drive in Birch Valley, and thought that was a good omen for involving Rochester. I put the paper into the folder, stood up and shook Hunter's hand. "Tomorrow's Saturday. I'll try and get over there then," I said. "Any suggestions on a good time to find her?"

"She's almost always there," Hunter said. "She's embarrassed to go out with that ankle bracelet, and she says it's too hot to wear long pants that would cover it up."

"Do you think either she or Carl were using drugs around the time he died?"

"I don't think so. The tox screens on Carl were negative for any drugs, and when they arrested Peggy they tested her, too, and she came up clean. I've seen her pretty frequently since then, and I don't see any evidence that she started using."

Hunter thanked me for my help, and I promised to get back to him. Then Rochester followed me out to the car, and we cut through a back exit to a farm road that would take us down to the Delaware, where I'd pick up the River Road that would take me to work.

I was surprised that Peggy had resisted my help, and wondered if she'd behaved the same way with Hunter Thirkell—or had they been closer than he was willing to admit? Maybe he was just a sucker for anyone in distress, as I often seemed to be. After all, that was how I'd come to adopt Rochester, when his human mom was murdered and I became determined to solve the crime and take him into my heart.

By the time I returned to Stewart's Crossing with my tail between my legs, one of my college professors at Eastern had become the chair of the English department, and he'd offered me an adjunct teaching gig. That began my second affiliation with the college. When a job came up in the alumni relations office where I could use my computer skills, he'd intervened with the hiring manager on my behalf.

That job had led to two things. Lili was the chair of the department of fine arts at Eastern, as well as a professor of photography, and we'd met at a big college fund-raiser and begun dating.

It had also brought me into close contact with the college president, who'd then tapped me to start up the college conference center at Friar Lake.

I was still mulling over the meeting with Hunter as Rochester and I drove up the River Road, then turned inland at the oak-lined switchback road that led up the hill to Friar Lake. An order of Catholic monks had built the complex of buildings, then known as Our Lady of the Waters, over a hundred years before, of local gray stone. When I started at the property, I supervised the renovation of the monks' dormitory into high-tech guest rooms, the conversion of the arched-roof chapel into a reception space, and the expansion of several of the outbuildings into classrooms.

My office was in the former gatehouse, and I pulled up in front of it and let Rochester out. In addition to developing and running executive education programs and enrichment seminars, I managed renting out the facility to companies and non-profit groups. That day we were hosting a continuing education seminar for psychologists who needed credits toward their state license renewal.

I left Rochester in my office with a rawhide bone, then walked along a cobblestone path to the largest classroom, where I turned on the lights, the computer and the projector. As I was fiddling with the air conditioning, Professor Andrea del Presto arrived.

She was in her late thirties, with long brown hair in a center part over a heart-shaped face. She had recently been granted tenure in the sociology department at Eastern, and her topic that day was "How and Why We Choose Our Partners," based on a research study she had done. We chatted for a couple of minutes as she logged into the college network and pulled up her presentation. Then I walked outside to where the maintenance staff had set up a registration table, and I showed the conference organizer how to access the college Wi-Fi network.

Then I returned to the classroom and stood in the back to listen to Professor del Presto's speech.

"My research began, as so many studies do, with a personal interest," she said. "When I was single, I went to see a psychologist to understand why I was choosing the men I was – none of whom ended up being right for me. She told me that deep inside, we understand the ways in which we need to change to make ourselves better, and we subconsciously choose partners who will make us change in that way."

I could see many of the therapists in the room nodding along with her. Had I done that? Looking back, I realized that

I was pretty directionless when I met Mary, and I was happy enough to climb on her express train as she moved forward with her career, then to marriage and our move to the West Coast.

But Lili? How had I needed to change when I met her, and had that change happened?

I tabled that thought as Professor del Presto brought up a slide and began to discuss her methodology. The science didn't interest me so my mind went back to the question of how Lili and I had become attracted to each other. There was the physical first; she was beautiful and sexy. She was smart and quick-witted, and our initial conversations fired on all cylinders.

But what did I need? I had been so scarred by Mary's miscarriages, and the demise of our marriage, that I had closed myself off from any thoughts of love. Then Rochester came into my life, and opened my heart again so that when I met Lili I was ready for her.

With two divorces behind her, she was happy to move as slowly as I was. Then over time, she showed me that a woman could be interested in a relationship without taking over, the way Mary had. Lili had forced me to assert myself when I needed to, without worrying that she would get angry and turn her back on me, the way Mary had done when I argued with her.

Lili had spent decades on the go from one country in trouble to the next, and the desire to change that pattern had driven her to take the job at Eastern, where she'd be rooted to a campus and a community. When she had the urge to move on, I comforted her with the knowledge that she could still travel and see the rest of the world while remaining in her job, in my townhouse with me and Rochester.

I looked out the window and saw a couple of guys on riding mowers moving across the broad lawns that bordered on the old stone buildings. My counterpart at Friar Lake was Joey Capodilupo, a tall, good-looking guy who managed the physical property, and I noticed he was talking to a man beside a roofer's truck. Even though we had done a major restoration of the property before it opened, there was always something that needed fixing—a good analogy for relationships, I thought.

The psychologists ate brown bag lunches in the restored chapel, then went into a smaller computer-equipped classroom to take a quiz on what they'd learned. By three o'clock they were gone, and I focused on answering college emails while Rochester dozed beside me. Joey came in to say hello, and Rochester jumped up, put his big paws on Joey's thighs, and nuzzled his groin.

I didn't have to apologize for the dog's behavior, though. Joey and his partner Mark had a golden retriever of their own, a big boy named Brody with a nearly pure-white coat. "Everything all right with the roof?" I asked.

"Yeah, just some minor work," he said, as he settled down across from me. "Listen, you're taking off for a week soon, aren't you?"

I nodded. "Lili found us an Airbnb cottage in Wildwood Crest, a block from the beach," I said. "Looking forward to going down the shore for a nice relaxing week."

"Can I take off after you get back? Mark and I are thinking of heading up to the Poconos. He has an Internet friend who runs a hotel in a little town up there."

"If you can manage without me for a week, I can do the same for you," I said. "You taking Brody with you?"

"Mark wouldn't part with him," Joey said. "He's become a total mother hen with that dog."

That was funny, since Joey had gotten Brody when he was single, and as far as I recalled Mark had been pretty reluctant to let a dog in his life, the way I had with Rochester. But then, Mark was an antiques dealer with shelves of fancy bric-a-brac in his home and store, and Brody was a force of nature with a big white plume of a tail that wagged dangerously.

Joey agreed to submit his vacation request into Eastern's online system, and I took Rochester out for a quick walk before leaving for home. I had known Mark first, and I was the one who'd introduced him to Joey. Mark had been shunned by his family when he came out, while Joey's experience had been the opposite. His father was the associate vice president of facilities for Eastern, and he'd mentored Joey with no problems about his son's orientation.

Mark wanted a family, and he got one with the effusive Capodilupo clan and with Brody as surrogate child. He and Joey melded well together, sharing interests in restoring old furniture and sniffing out bargains at flea markets. Meeting a solid, relationship-oriented guy like Mark had helped Joey see that he could have a life like his parents had, when all he'd known of dating before was clubs and hookups in Philadelphia.

Professor del Presto knew her stuff, I thought, as I loaded Rochester into the car and we headed for home. What would she make of Peggy Doyle? How did the dancer at Club Hott need to change, and how had Carl Landsea pushed her? I would be interested to see her and figure that out.

On the surface, it looked like Carl Landsea provided her with a stable home life and a way out of dancing. But if that anonymous caller was right, Carl had been abusive. Had

Peggy's desire to have a man look after her backfired?

I was still fascinated to know how the girl who had been so kind to me, so determined to succeed on her own terms, had gotten so far off track.

# 4 – No Angels

Rochester and I were halfway down the River Road on the way to Stewart's Crossing when Rick called. "Last minute opportunity for a sleepover at Tamsen's tonight," he said. "Can you take Rascal?"

Rascal was the Australian shepherd Rick had found at a shelter a few months after I took in Rochester, and the two dogs were bosom buddies. I knew Lili wouldn't mind having Rascal for the evening; he was no trouble, because he and Rochester usually played like crazy for a while and then collapsed together on the floor.

Rick had been scarred by his divorce, too, but his fundamental personality trait was to be a caretaker. That's why he had gone into police work, and that was what had attracted him to his fiancée, Tamsen Morgan. She was a widow with a young son, and looked on the surface like someone who needed to be taken care of.

Pretty quickly, she had demonstrated to Rick that she was self-sufficient. She had a successful business and was doing a great job of raising her boy. Rick had been forced to learn that he could have a relationship with a woman who didn't need a man to tell her what to do, and she'd come to rely on him to help her when she requested it.

I made plans for him to drop off Rascal, then called Lili to let her know. She didn't feel like cooking dinner so suggested I pick up hoagies for us at DeLorenzo's in the center of Stewart's Crossing. I took her order – a foot-long teriyaki chicken on white, with mushrooms and extra teriyaki sauce. I left Rochester in the car with the windows open while I went inside and ordered her sandwich and mine, a foot-long turkey breast on white, with extra turkey breast on the side for Rochester. I splurged on a six-pack of Frank's black cherry wishniak soda, smiling as I remembered their slogan from my childhood: "Is it Frank's? Thanks!"

I brought the food home, and as we ate, I told Lili about Professor del Presto's study, and I wanted to see if she shared my opinions about what had attracted us, and kept us together. "Do you think I've made you change in a way you needed to?" I asked.

She looked up at me, her head tilted. "I was so tired of running when I met you," she said. "From marriage to marriage, from assignment to assignment, country to country. I just wanted to settle down. Seeing you, your connections to Stewart's Crossing, the way you felt so grounded here—that appealed to me."

She picked up her hoagie again. "And I know you haven't been happy when I've picked up the occasional freelance job that takes me away, but you haven't complained, and you've made me feel like I always have you to come home to." She smiled. "How about you?"

"I've been trying to figure that out," I said. "I certainly knew somewhere deep down that I had to stop hacking, and I needed someone who'd hold me accountable."

"So you saw me as what, a dominatrix?" Lili's eyes danced and I knew she was joking — even if only in part.

"No. More like I admired how much you had accomplished, and I wanted to make myself worthy of you."

"That's sweet," she said.

"And when I do get caught up in something, I always have you as an angel on my shoulder, appealing to my best side. Like if I do anything to help Peggy Landsea, I know that I won't risk anything that would get me in trouble or cause me to lose what I have here with you and Rochester."

As if he'd recognized his name, the big golden suddenly jumped up, raced to the front door and started barking. "What's up with you, dog?"

I looked out the window and didn't see anyone there. But a moment later, Rick's truck came around the corner. How did the dog do that? Did he have extra-sharp hearing or just a sixth sense about the approach of his best friend?

I opened the gate as Rick got out of the truck, and

Rascal didn't wait to have the other door opened for him – the big black and white dog trampled on his dad and jumped out the driver's side, racing up to Rochester. The two of them turned on their heels and ran inside, where I could hear their toenails scrabbling up the staircase to the second floor.

Rick was my age, but his short hair was grayer than mine, and he was slimmer and more fit. We had shared a chemistry class at Pennsbury High during our senior year, and then reconnected after I returned to town, bonding over our divorces. Then he'd adopted Rascal, and our friendship had been cemented through our dogs.

"Hannah and Eric offered to take Justin to the movies with Nathaniel tonight," he said, as he walked in. "With sleepover to follow."

Hannah was Tamsen's sister, and I could see she was doing her best to move the relationship between Rick and Tamsen along. "And so you get a sleepover, too."

Rick's grin was broad. "I do."

"You have a minute before you have to go? I wanted to ask you a question."

"I never like it when you start conversations like that, but sure, Hannah's not picking up Justin for a half hour, and I don't want to be hovering at the end of the street like some perv, waiting for the pretty lady to be all alone in her house."

"TMI," I said. I led him into the living room, where Lili greeted him and said she'd be upstairs making sure the dogs didn't destroy anything. We could hear them racing around from room to room, jumping on and off the furniture up there.

I sat on the couch, and Rick slid into the chair across from me. I told him that I'd agreed to help Hunter Thirkell with Peggy's case. "Did you know Peggy Doyle in high school?" I asked.

"Different circles," he said. "I was already thinking about becoming a cop so I tried to stay away from anybody who might belong to FFA."

"Future Farmers of America?" Our school district encompassed a lot of rural areas where kids were on their way to take over family farms — though most of those farms had ended up being sold to real estate developers instead of being handed down.

"No, doofus. Future Felons of America. A joke."

"Yeah, I'm sure Peggy will think that's a howler. Why would you think that? She was a super achiever in high school."

"I knew one of her sisters from study hall and she was a wild child. I just assumed Peggy was like that, too."

"Peggy was the exact opposite." I told him about my friendship with Peggy, cemented by foreign travel and college courses. "See, here's the thing," I said. "I can't make that old picture I have of her square with the way people are describing her today. I want to do what I can to help her."

Though the case didn't have anything to do with the Stewart's Crossing department, Rick was familiar with it because of all the media coverage.

"He asked me to see if I can get into her last husband's email account, because he thinks there may be information there that would lead to additional suspects."

"Would that help involve your nimble fingers dancing over a keyboard and then taking a dive into the deep web?"

"No, nothing illegal." I was impressed by Rick's analogy. He was usually a much more straightforward thinker. I guessed hanging around with Tamsen, a marketing wizard, was improving his thought processes.

Or maybe it was me who was doing that for him.

"Hunter says that as Carl Landsea's heir, Peggy has the authority to look at anything he left behind, and she can delegate that to Hunter, her attorney. In turn, he authorizes me, and it's all legit."

I leaned forward. "Have you ever heard of a motorcycle gang called Levitt's Angels?"

"I'm a cop. Of course I have." Rick frowned. "When you snoop into motorcycle gangs, you're getting into some dangerous shit, Steve. I know from past experience you never listen to my advice, but tread carefully, okay?"

"I listen to you," I protested.

"And then you end up doing what you want anyway." He sighed deeply. "So here's the quick take on the Angels, who of course are no angels at all."

"Irony," I said.

"College professor."

"Hey, I yam who I yam," I said, quoting the Popeye cartoons we had both loved as kids. "So how devilish are they?"

"They're not as bad as some of the other biker dudes they hang around with, the Hell's Angels, the Pagans and the Outlaws. Those dudes are into murder, extortion and arson—anything criminal they can make money on. The Levitts are not exactly law-abiding, but they the worst thing I've heard about them is that last year they had a big bust-up with a branch of the Warlords outside a dive bar off of US 1 in Northeast Philly."

Rochester and Rascal came over and nuzzled him, one on each side. "The bar got trashed and there were arrests for drunk and disorderly conduct," he continued, "but surprisingly, no one was willing to say what the fight was about. Rumor had it, though, that the Warlords thought the

Levitts were breaching walls into their territory. Since then the Levitts have been keeping a low profile. Though individual members may have records or ongoing cases, and I don't know of any open investigations against the group as a whole right now."

Rochester got tired of sharing Rick's attention and came over to me, and Rascal slumped on the floor in front of his dad.

"Can you suggest anyone I can talk to about them?" I asked. "A cop from another area?" Rochester nuzzled my leg and I scratched behind his ear.

"No. And that would be *N, O.* I'm not going to enable you."

More psych language. It must be catching.

I held up my hands. "No worries. I'm not doing anything that could get me in trouble."

"Yeah, right. Like I said before, just tread carefully."

He left a short while later, and when the dogs went upstairs to Lili, I pulled out the folder Hunter had given me and began to read the articles he'd printed, most of which centered on that big fight between the two gangs that Rick had mentioned.

The tone of the articles from the *Courier-Times* and the Philadelphia *Inquirer* was inflammatory, beginning with background on the Warlords, who were as bad as Rick had said, if not worse. Members were suspected of involvement with drug dealing, trafficking in stolen goods, and coercing immigrant women from Eastern Europe into prostitution.

Some of the material was almost silly. One article speculated that a rise in tax on soda in Philadelphia had led to the Warlords getting involved in smuggling untaxed carbonated beverages into the city. I thought of the black cherry wishniak I'd bought at Lorenzo's and wondered if all the proper taxes had been paid on it.

The Levitts, on the other hand, got little ink, because the reporters dismissed them as a group of wannabes who'd gotten on the wrong side of the real bad guys. And after a few days without anything new, the story died out.

And yet Rick had believed that the bar brawl had been because the Angels were trying to snatch some illegal dollars away from the Warlords. I'd trust him over a headline-seeking reporter, which meant I had to tread carefully.

All Hunter had been able to dig up was that collection of articles. But then, he didn't have my internet skills, and I turned to my laptop. I found a number of small mentions of the group, mostly in lists of outlaw biker gangs, and by digging through some databases I reached through Eastern's college library, I found one in-depth article from several years back.

According to the author, a reporter for a crime-focused website, the club's growth and development was closely tied to that of Levittown. Motorcycle clubs, I learned, had their roots in the immediate post-World War II era of American society. Members rode cruiser motorcycles, particularly Harley-Davidsons and choppers, and they were fueled by a set of ideals that celebrated freedom, nonconformity to mainstream culture and loyalty to the biker group.

Levittown was the very definition of conformity back when it was built. There were only six original house models, from the Country Clubber to the Jubilee, and the meandering streets were confusing. My father used to tell a joke about a guy who lived in Levittown, who parked in the wrong driveway, went into the wrong house and had dinner with the wrong family, because the houses all looked alike and the neighborhoods were so cookie-cutter.

At least that's the version he told when I was a kid. As I grew up, he expanded it to add that the guy made love to the wrong wife, too.

I could see how someone who was rebelling against the conformity of Levittown would be drawn to such a group. Levitt's Angels were a smaller group than many, and for a couple of decades they'd focused on small-time crime like protection and prostitution. Several of the members had been arrested for smash-and-grab thefts at small computer stores, though none of them had gotten prison time, and Carl Landsea's name wasn't among those who were charged.

That was all I could find. My hands were poised over the keyboard as I thought about where to look next, and I remembered what Rick had said about taking a dive into the deep web.

I often heard cyber guys compare the Internet to an iceberg. Only about ten percent of all networked material is accessible through search engines and web crawlers. Techies call that the surface web.

Material like your bank account information, email folders, corporate intranets and so on—anything that you need a password to access–is called the deep web. These don't show up in a search engine, and you wouldn't want them to.

There is another part of that submerged iceberg, called the dark web. And that's where criminals lurk, selling consumer information, trafficking in drugs, sharing kiddie porn and so on. It's not illegal to sniff around there, but because most people who were there were in search of illicit materials or connections, I had to tread carefully. I didn't want my computer's unique IP address to pop up in some police search and cause authorities to come looking at me. Even though I wasn't doing anything wrong, I had skirted the law in the past and I didn't want to invite scrutiny of my habits.

I had sworn to Rick and Lili that I would resist the urge to hack just because I could, and because I was determined not to jeopardize the new life I'd found with Lili and Rochester. Besides, Hunter could only use information I found legitimately in his defense of Peggy.

So instead of hacking, I'd talk to Peggy. Surely she knew that her husband was no angel, even though I didn't think she and Carl had been married when he was arrested the last time. Hunter had already given me permission to access Carl's email account, but I needed Peggy to share details with me that would help me figure out his password legitimately, like his childhood addresses and phone numbers and other words or numbers that had personal meaning to him.

If she'd see me, that is.

# 5 – Starting Over

Saturday morning, after taking the dogs on a long walk around River Bend, I was in the middle of fixing French toast for Lili and me for breakfast when Rick showed up. It didn't take much to convince him to stick around and join us. Maybe it was the company, but more likely it was the smell of the cinnamon and the rich challah bread.

"Kids get up so damn early," he complained as he slid into a chair at our kitchen table. Lili passed him the carton of orange juice, and I handed him a glass. "It was eight o'clock and Hannah called to give Tamsen a heads-up that Justin was ready to come home."

"Any idea when you're going to let Justin know you and his mom are getting serious?"

He shrugged. "If it was up to me, I'd have said something already. But Tamsen's understandably concerned. I'm already his football coach and she's afraid that if he gets too close to me, and we break up, it'll hit him hard."

"Kids are resilient," I said. "Look at Peggy Doyle. She grew up in the slums, lost her father, then bounced back to be a great student in high school, work her way into that trip to France."

"I don't think I want to point out the Black Widow of

Birch Valley as a role model for Justin," Rick said.

"Enough negative talk at breakfast," Lili said. "What did you and Tamsen do last night...I mean, beyond the obvious."

"We got a last minute reservation at Le Canal," he said. It was a fancy French restaurant upriver in New Hope where we'd all gone on occasion.

"Good choice," Lili said. "It was pretty clear night last night, wasn't it?"

"It was. Lots of stars out. We walked along the towpath after dinner for a while, just holding hands."

"That sounds lovely and romantic."

There was something in her tone that made me think romance might be lacking in our own relationship. "I'll bet we can see stars at Wildwood Crest," I said, reminding her of our upcoming getaway.

"You sure can," Rick said, jumping to my defense.

"Assuming Steve actually makes it to the shore," Lili said. "Instead of staying back here tilting at windmills and websites."

"Come on. This vacation was my idea. I am totally looking forward to spending a lot of quality time with you."

"We'll see," she said darkly.

Rick finished his French toast and summoned Rascal to

his truck. Then Lili left soon after for a mani-pedi appointment with one of her friends from the Eastern faculty, and I piled Rochester into my aged BMW sedan for the trip over to Peggy Landsea's. He had a talent for getting people to like him, and if Peggy was going to be reluctant to talk to me, maybe Rochester could woo her over.

Despite the word "town" in its name, Levittown isn't actually a town. Instead, it's a cluster of forty-one different neighborhoods sprawled over four different municipalities and three school districts. Each of the divisions has a name, from Appletree Hill to Yellowwood, and within that community all the streets begin with the same letter. For some developments, such as Quincy Hollow and Upper Orchard, that was a good thing — if someone lived on Quaint or Quail, you knew where you were going in the twenty-two square miles of developments.

Fortunately, I already knew that Bark Road was in Birch Valley, otherwise I might have wondered if it was in the other "B" neighborhood, Blue Ridge. Most of the neighborhoods had that kind of pastoral name, referencing plants like violet, forsythia and juniper, and natural features like hollow, brook and orchard.

The reality was grimmer. There were no orange trees in Orangewood, no ponds in Elderberry Pond. Just an endless maze of houses and yards, most of them customized far away from the original structures with carports, faux-stone facades and attached mother-in-law suites.

Birch Valley looked like most of the Levittown neighborhoods I'd visited. Lawns strewn with kids' toys, driveways jammed with every kind of car from old beaters to brand-new Mercedes. Bark Road was a long, curving street of single-story and split-level homes, and even if I hadn't known the address I could have picked out Peggy's—it was the one with the weedy yard, peeling paint and broken window shutter.

I parked in the driveway behind a battered old Nissan compact in the carport. Rochester followed me out my door, and immediately made a beeline for a dying magnolia tree, where he peed copiously.

The woman who appeared at the screen door looked older than I expected, but I recognized her anyway. She had a few more lines on her forehead and there was some gray in her hair but underneath I saw the girl I'd known.

"Steve?" she said, and I could tell her voice had hoarsened over the years, and sounded like she'd had her share of tobacco and alcohol along the way.

"In the flesh," I said. "And this is Rochester. Can we come in?"

She shook her head. "I told Hunter I didn't want to talk to you."

"Why not? I know I didn't keep up with you after I went to college. I'm sorry, but you know, that's a two-way street. You had my parents' address and phone number and I never heard from you either."

"I was so envious of you," she said, fiddling with a loose hair that refused to stay tucked behind her ear. "Going to a real college, while I was stuck at BC3. Can you blame me for not wanting to hear about how great your life was going?"

"Well, it didn't work out that well," I said. "One failed marriage, a year in the California penal system, and then two years back here on probation."

Peggy's mouth opened in surprise. "You went to prison? But you were so smart."

"Yeah, too smart for my own good is what my probation officer used to say."

I could see Peggy wavering.

"I served my time for computer hacking, in case Hunter didn't share that with you. So I know something about computers and retrieving deleted emails. You were kind to me when we were kids, Peggy. Let me do something for you in return."

She frowned, and then looked down at Rochester,

sitting on his butt so politely waiting to be invited in. "You used to have a poodle when we were kids, didn't you?" Peggy said. "I guess you upsized."

"You could say that. Rochester's very sweet."

She opened the screen door. "You might as well come in then."

Rochester rose but instead of scampering inside immediately he stopped by Peggy so she could pet him and he could sniff her.

Peggy had never been a pretty girl, but she'd made up for her freckles, lackluster brown hair and offset eyes with a bubbly personality. She wasn't so cheerful anymore, but the big change was that the slim, almost boyish physique I remembered had been artificially enhanced. Her breasts had gone up a few cup sizes, and she'd probably had work done on her butt as well.

Focus, I told myself as Rochester and I followed her inside.

"I heard the basics of your situation from Hunter," I said, once I sat down on a big leather couch in the living room, with Rochester at my feet. Peggy sat with her legs crossed under her on a recliner across from me, and I saw the ankle bracelet that kept track of her movements. "He wants me to see if I can retrieve the emails that you say Carl deleted from his account."

"The lawyers always talk like that," Peggy said. "That I 'say' he deleted. Like it's not true, just something I'm saying."

"And that's all I've got to go on," I said. "For now, I'm taking it on faith that these emails exist. I believe you, because I know the person you were back then." I pulled a small notebook out of my pocket. "I'm going to need as much information as you can give me about Carl so I can try to figure out his password."

We went through all the basic data—his birthdate, the day they were married, and so on. I got as much information as she could provide. "The police took his laptop computer, right?" I asked. "No desktop?"

"Just the laptop."

So much for getting my hands on the actual hardware.

She stood up. "He had an address book somewhere. Let me see if I can find it."

While she searched, I looked around. The house was neat but dusty, as if someone had cleaned it up and then gone away for a while. I imagined that was because Peggy was either grieving for Carl, or worried about her own future, or both.

The furniture was old-fashioned upholstered wood, and the cushions on the leather recliner had sagged. No books, which surprised me, because Peggy had been a big reader when we were kids.

Maybe she kept those upstairs in her bedroom. I hoped she hadn't given up on the escape that books could provide – reading had helped me get through prison, and then the lonely months after I returned to Stewart's Crossing, before Rochester came into my life.

Peggy opened a big armoire made of distressed wood and began to sift through the junk inside. Rochester got up and stood beside her as she looked, and in between moving papers and folders around, she petted his head. "Here it is," she said.

She closed the doors to the armoire and crossed the room, Rochester hard on her heels. She handed me a small leather-bound address book that looked like Carl had owned it for much of his life. Names and addresses had been crossed through, updated and crossed through again. But it was quite readable, and might give me the clues I needed.

"You think you can do anything?" Peggy asked as she sat across from me again. Rochester stayed beside her, as if he knew she needed his love. "I know Carl was into some bad shit with the Levitts, but none of them will talk to me."

"I'm going to plug all this information into some software I have that generates passwords. The program will keep spitting out possible choices and trying them on Carl's account. I know from past experience this email provider keeps everything archived on their servers for as long as you have your account. With some luck, I'll be able to get in there and see what's in his trash folder."

"And if you can't get in?"

"I have some other alternatives," I said, and I felt that familiar tingle in my fingertips that came when I was about to break into some site where I wasn't supposed to be. Rochester sat up and sniffed my hand, and I wondered if thinking about hacking set off some endorphins in my brain that he could sense or smell.

"I've got enough to get started," I said. Then I looked over at Peggy. I couldn't believe that she'd tampered with her husband's brakes. "Who do you think killed Carl?"

Peggy's posture sagged, as if she was remembering all over again that her husband was dead, her mouth turned down at the edges and her eyelids drooped. She took a couple of deep breaths to center herself, then looked up at me.

"I'm not even sure someone killed him. Carl was always working on his bike, and I think it's possible that he screwed up the brakes without realizing it when he was working on something else. He tried to show me how the bike worked a couple of times but I was never interested enough to pay much attention. But I know all those wires are interconnected."

I nodded. "And you told the police and Hunter that?"

"Nobody listens to me," she said. She faced down, her back bent, and body language closed. I knew enough to interpret that as serious depression.

"I'm listening," I said. "Any other ideas?"

She looked up, her lips pursed, her eyes intent. Finally, she said, "I figure it had to be one of his biker buddies. They were always drinking too much and getting in trouble. That's why I wanted to see Carl's emails. See if they were planning a crime and maybe they were worried Carl was going to rat them out. He did that once. Turned over on another of the bikers."

"You know the guy's name?"

"Frank. But he had some other name in the gang, some kind of dumb pun. I only heard it once or twice so I don't remember."

"I'll keep an eye out for one of the Levitt's Angels named Frank," I said. "I'm curious, though. They used email instead of texting each other?"

Peggy snorted. "Carl still had one of those old flip phones," she said. "He said his fingers were too big and he was too old to get into texting."

I let her think about other suspects for a while, but she couldn't come up with anyone else, so eventually I stood up. "I'll keep in touch and let you know when I make progress."

* * *

When I got home Lili was out, and I was glad she wasn't there to see me retrieve the ladder from the garage and carry it up to the second floor. She'd know immediately what I was doing, and I wasn't ready to tell her everything yet.

I set the ladder up in the hallway outside the second bathroom and climbed up, pushing away the hatch that led to the attic crawl space, where I kept my secret laptop.

It wasn't quite so secret as it had been – Rick and Lili both knew that it existed, and that I kept the hacking tools on it up to date, even though I didn't use them. But I stored it in the attic so it wasn't easy for me to turn to it.

It had once belonged to Caroline Kelly, Rochester's first mom, and after she died I loaded my hacking tools on it and used what I learned online to help Rick figure out who killed her.

Since then I had used the tools there occasionally, for the most part in legal pursuits.

I closed up the attic and returned the ladder to the garage. While I waited for the old laptop to boot up, I thought about the legality of what I was doing. I was no lawyer, but I had studied up on the technicalities of hacking over the years. Because Peggy was Carl Landsea's legal heir for the time being, she had the authority over his possessions, including access to his electronic data, and she had willingly granted that access to Hunter, and then to me.

It also was not illegal for me to try and figure out Carl's password and gain access to his email, because I was doing it under Peggy's authority.

At least, that's the way I read the law, and I was going with that interpretation. I turned on my regular laptop and logged into a database I subscribed to, that promised to find out everything about everybody, from past addresses to family connections to criminal records. I plugged in "Carl Landsea" and began adding to the information that Peggy had given me.

Carl had been born in Bristol, a few miles downriver from Stewart's Crossing. He was a few years older than I was, and I figured out that he'd graduated from Pennsbury High like Peggy, Rick and I had. Carl had a spotty employment record, or at least the software only provided a couple of jobs, from the Fairless Works steel mill to his last job at a bike shop called Pennsy Choppers in Tullytown, one of the municipalities that included parts of Levittown.

He had four connections to other people—a woman

who I assumed was his mother, who had died some years before, a sister named Charlene Landsea Brattain, an ex-wife named Miriam Coyne Landsea, and Peggy herself.

I kept searching, finding an address in Bristol where I thought he'd grown up, and an old phone number. I added all that information to the keywords and numbers to my list.

Carl also had numerous felony and misdemeanor convictions, but I saved that information into a file for future reference. When I was finally confident I'd found out everything I could about him, I turned back to Caroline's laptop and chose one of my password cracking tools, one which was commonly used to perform what were called dictionary attacks. It took text string samples from a file called a wordlist, containing popular and complex words found in a dictionary as well as real passwords cracked before. I was able to add all Carl's information to the wordlist as well. Because it used its own database, it could be called an offline password cracker, as opposed to one that looked for data online.

I plugged in all the data I had, and then I opened a connection to Carl's email provider, a free service called MyEMail.com. As with most secure sites these days, the server at MyEMail.com had installed a program that kicked you out after too many password attempts. Fortunately, my password software had a feature that got around that, though it meant the connection was cut every three tries and had to restart. I could see it was going to take some time, so I got up and made myself a café mocha.

Rochester was on me like a fly on a pile of shit, following me to the kitchen, then back to the dining room where the laptop was still working. I watched for a few minutes as Google Chrome opened up the log-in page for MyEMail.com, auto-filled Carl's address, then threw in a potential password. After three tries, the MyEmail.com server put up an error message, and my software shut down the browser, then opened it afresh and reconnected to the log-in page.

It was mesmerizing to watch the software try and fail to get into Carl's account, then start over again when pushed.

Kind of like my life. Starting over when pushed.

# 6 – Bad Guys and Trouble

While I waited for the password software to come up with the right combination, I turned back to my regular laptop and looked at the police records I'd found for Carl Landsea. Maybe I could find information there that would lead Hunter toward a different suspect for Carl's murder.

Carl had three arrests for disorderly conduct, a "summary offense" in Pennsylvania. That meant it was a less serious charge than a felony or misdemeanor, and not a criminal conviction.

The most recent of the arrests, though, had been prosecuted as a third degree misdemeanor. Carl had escaped prison time but had been fined a thousand dollars.

Then I found two arrests for "Possession of other Controlled Substances Penalties (Heroin, Cocaine, LSD/Acid, Ecstasy/MMDA, Meth, and prescription drugs including Vicodin and Oxycontin or illegal steroids)."

That was a lot more serious, and I did a quick look up for the penalties involved in such crimes. For a first offense, Carl could have received up to a year in prison with a $5,000 fine, while a second offense generated the same fine but added an additional year in prison. From what I could tell, however, the first arrest had been dropped, and Carl had pled out to another fine and "time served" for the second.

I couldn't tell from the government database I was using, one that was open to the public, whether Carl had been using the drugs himself, or just selling them.

Carl's situation was typical of many of the guys I'd met in prison. Most of them had been arrested multiple times, on increasingly serious offenses, before they'd actually served time, and even then, they'd made plea deals or gotten early release that limited their actual time in prison.

The prosecutor in my case had tried to get me a five-year sentence, but the judge had reduced that two years because of my emotional state at the time of the crime – my attorney argued that because of the effect on me of Mary's miscarriages, I wasn't thinking clearly. For good behavior, and because the California penal system was undergoing one of its periodic purges, I'd spent only one year inside.

Carl's record showed he wasn't exactly a Boy Scout— though given what the press had revealed about the discriminatory practices of that organization, the cliché had ceased to have any real meaning.

When Lili came home, I jumped up to help her bring in groceries as Rochester danced around her. "I saw some gorgeous eggplant at the farmer's market," she said. "I thought we'd make eggplant parmigiana for dinner."

"And by we, you mean me," I said.

"It is your favorite recipe."

"That's true. And I'm glad to make it for you."

She kissed me on the lips. "That's sweet. I thought I might take Rochester out for a walk along the canal and take some pictures. The college finally came through with some funds to buy new cameras for student use, and I want to get a handle on the features myself before I hand them over."

"What kind of camera?"

"It's a new Panasonic model, with interchangeable lenses and a 20 megapixel sensor. It also has a high resolution viewfinder that tilts, so I can take some selfies with Rochester if I want."

I was a bit jealous she was going off with the dog, leaving me home to cook, but I reminded myself that we were a family of three — Lili, Rochester and me — and if she wanted to take selfies with the dog it just meant that she loved him.

"I'm glad you're so excited," I said. "You take the dog, and I'll get started on the eggplant."

She either didn't notice the extra laptop on the dining room table, or she didn't mention it. Rochester did his usual happy dance when he heard the clatter of his leash, though he did look back at me in confusion when he realized I wasn't going with him and Lili.

I checked the password generator and it was still making its three tries then rebooting, so I began slicing and breading the eggplant, then sautéing it. The quiet repetitive work helped me focus on my ideas about Peggy Landsea.

Could she be innocent? I wanted to believe it, because I knew the girl she had been, and I had already found evidence that Carl Landsea was a bad guy. And when we spoke about Carl, she genuinely seemed to be mourning him. From my experience in prison, I knew that bad guys attracted trouble, in the form of other bad guys, and that meant there might be other suspects in Carl's death.

Hunter was only interested in developing reasonable doubt that Peggy was guilty, but I realized that I wanted more – I wanted to know who killed Carl, and why.

That was just the kind of fascination that had gotten me in trouble in the past.

I finished preparing the eggplant parmigiana, layering the fried slices with mozzarella cheese, mushrooms and tomato sauce, and slid the casserole into the oven to bake.

For a while, I sat at the laptop in the dining room, mesmerized by the constant stream of possible passwords on the screen. I let my mind wander back to the Peggy I had known as a kid.

She was always so enthusiastic, never letting on how

her difficult childhood had affected her. Her sisters weren't quite so cheerful, though, and I remembered meeting her baby sister RJ once. One night toward the end of the semester Peggy's car broke down and I was able to borrow my dad's car and drive us up to class. I went over to Peggy's house to pick her up, and RJ, who had to be eleven or twelve, kept dancing around the car, calling Peggy "college girl" teasingly.

"Your sister must be proud that you're going to college," I said, as we drove away.

"She's not, really. I'm the first one in my family to go to college and she's just imitating some of my relatives who think I'm getting above myself," she said.

My parents had always pushed me to go to college, so I admired Peggy so much then for her tenacity. I couldn't reconcile the girl she had been with the Black Widow of Birch Valley.

Suddenly, the password generator found the right log in combination, and Carl's online mailbox popped up on the screen. I was in! I wrote down the password – a version of Carl's childhood address mixed with special characters. Then I turned to the list of emails that had come in since his death.

I'd deleted a dozen spam message by the time I heard Lili's car pull up in the driveway. I quickly saved Carl's password to the laptop's desktop, then shut everything down.

Then the timer on the oven began to ring, signaling that the eggplant parmigiana was done. When Lili and Rochester came in, I was in the kitchen pulling the casserole from the oven.

"How'd the photo session go?" I asked, as Rochester romped over to me and tried to stick his nose into the casserole.

"I'm impressed that that this camera has a Leica rangefinder, because I used them for years when I was a photojournalist. If it's as good as I think it is I might use the rest of the money I have to buy a Leica 8-18mm lens which students can use for landscape, cityscape and street pictures. There's also a great portrait lens also designed by Leica that I can use in the school studio to teach portrait lighting techniques."

It struck me that Lili spouted off the technical specs for the camera the way I babbled about computers and hacking software. The passion for our interests was something else we had in common.

We talked more about the camera as we ate, and then, because I cooked, Lili volunteered to clean up. While I helped her ferry the dirty dishes to the sink, I mentioned that Peggy had asked me to retrieve the deleted emails from Carl's account.

She frowned.

"It's all legal," I said. I repeated what I had told Rick about Peggy's authority to access anything Carl left behind, and the way she had authorized me to act on her behalf.

"I thought she was accused of killing him. How can she be his heir under those circumstances?"

"Innocent until proven guilty," I said.

"And what happens if she does get convicted? Does that put you in a bad position?"

I shook my head. "Not according to Hunter, and he's the attorney. I'm also working at his direction, so anything I do is covered under attorney-client privilege."

"Even though you're not the client."

I struggled not to get irritated. Lili was only looking out for me. "Anything I do at either her direction or Hunter's comes under that same protection."

She sighed. "I said it before and I'll say it again. I trust you. And I'm glad you told me what you're doing."

I leaned over and kissed her. "I love you, too, and I'm sticking to my promise not to do anything to jeopardize our relationship."

She began washing the dishes, and I went back to my hacker laptop on the dining room table. I sent Hunter a quick email letting him know that I had made contact with Peggy, and was working on retrieving Carl's emails. Then I opened up Carl's account and quickly downloaded the new messages to a file I saved on my jump drive.

It felt creepy logging into a dead man's account, and I was pleased that my fingers didn't tingle the way they usually did when I was digging somewhere I didn't belong. Maybe it was that I had the right to be there — or maybe I was learning.

After the file downloaded, I checked the Trash folder in Carl's email account. He must not have been all that savvy, because everything he had deleted from years before his death was still stored there. Once again, I downloaded the data and saved it to a file. My stomach felt weird and my anxiety level was high, so I was glad when I had all the data and I was able to log out.

When I first promised Lili and Rick to stop hacking, or at least control my impulses, I had joined an online support group for hackers, and I logged into it then. I wanted to see if anyone else had experienced similar feelings while doing something ostensibly legal.

A couple of the regulars had dropped out, either because they could control themselves on their own, or because they had backslid. I hadn't been that active myself because I wasn't having too many problems.

No one was online at the moment, so I made a post in which I described in general terms what I'd done, and how I'd felt. "Anyone else feel this way? Is this progress?"

Lili was sitting on the couch by then, reading, and I shut down the laptop and joined her there with my Kindle. I'd always been a big mystery reader, but over the last few months I'd developed more of a taste for historical work. It was a relief to read something that no connection to computers, social media or hacking. At the moment I was reading a mystery set in Rome just before Julius Caesar was murdered on the Ides of March, and I was eagerly moving forward to see how the author would incorporate the historical detail with his own plot.

We read together for a while, with Rochester sprawled on the floor beside us, and I pushed away all thoughts of Peggy Landsea and computer hacking. At one point I looked up to see Lili engrossed in her book, and I realized how lucky I was to have found her.

As if he knew what I was thinking, Rochester got up on his haunches and sniffed my hand. "You too, boy," I said, continuing out loud the discussion in my head. "Always you, too."

Lili looked up but didn't say anything, just smiled, and went back to her book.

* * *

Sunday morning as we finished a breakfast of lox and

eggs, Lili announced that she wanted to go out and take more pictures with the new camera. "You don't mind, do you?" she asked. "It's such a beautiful day and I want to experiment with different light levels."

"Go right ahead," I said. "I'm going to start looking through all the messages I downloaded from Carl Landsea's email account."

She went upstairs to get dressed, and though she kissed me on the cheek on her way out, I was already ankle deep in Carl Landsea's email account.

I began with the file of recent messages. Almost all of them were junk, as though his personal contacts had known of his death, but for a few weeks he got regular email updates from the Levitt's Angels email list until someone manually removed him.

None of those messages were very interesting — mostly questions about technical problems or suggestions for places to ride. I hadn't expected to see any mention of criminal activity — even the dumbest cons these days knew enough to keep things out of writing. I did manage to collect the names and email addresses of a half-dozen other Angels. I wasn't sure what I'd do with them, but I created a spreadsheet and input that data, which at least gave me the illusion that I was making progress.

After about an hour, I got antsy. The work ahead of me was boring and tedious, and I wanted to do something active. I looked over at Rochester, the way he was splayed on the floor facing me, his front paws flat on the floor and I had a momentary image of him riding a motorcycle that way.

"Biker dog," I said to him, and laughed.

He looked up at me as if he didn't understand, and I held my hands out as if I was gripping handlebars and said, "Vroom, vroom!"

He jumped up and came over to me, and I laughed again and petted him. But that image of him as a biker dog resonated with me, and I let my brain make the connections. Was there anything I could about Carl by exploring his biker connections?

I'd been interested in riding a motorcycle since I was in my teens, when all the bad boys did, but my friends were all nerdy college-bound kids like I was and no one knew anyone who rode a bike.

As a student at Eastern the only person who rode a motorcycle that I was aware of was an older professor in the religion department, with a mane of white hair. He certainly wasn't the kind of guy I could go up to and ask for a ride—not unless I wanted a lecture on the history of world religions.

Then I'd moved to Manhattan, where everyone I knew

stuck to public transportation. When I moved to California, though, I worked for a small web startup for a couple of years, where I learned most of my hacking skills. Many of the guys were younger than I was, and our boss was into group bonding exercises.

One year, he decided he wanted us all to learn to ride motorcycles, and take a trip together up the Pacific Coast Highway to Big Sur, where he rented a big house and where we'd have group sessions about our goals for the following year.

He paid for those of us who didn't have motorcycle licenses to take the 15-hour training course and gain our learners' permits, and he was right—it was a good bonding exercise for the six of us who took it together. A couple of the guys were married, too, and their wives expressed some concern about them on bikes—but Mary had no complaints.

It was about six months after her first miscarriage, so maybe her lack of interest was a sign that she didn't care as much about me by then. Or maybe she simply had a lot more on her mind, monitoring her period and telling me exactly when we had to have sex and in what position in order to maximize the potential of getting pregnant.

With my permit in hand, I rode with the group up to Big Sur. It was scary, navigating those curves and narrow lanes, but exhilarating, too.

I probably would have gone on to get my regular license, except Mary had her second miscarriage and everything changed for us. But now? Maybe it was time to get that license, have some fun before I got too old. I'd be a good biker, observing the speed limits, maybe joining in those poker runs to raise money for handicapped children.

Somehow I had difficulty imagining Carl Landsea or the Levitt's Angels doing that, but my exposure to the prison population had changed my attitudes about a lot of things and broadened my outlook. Maybe it was time I got back on a bike. I'd see if I still enjoyed it, and if talking to bikers could help me find out what had happened to Carl.

# 7 – Pennsy Choppers

I looked up the address for Pennsy Choppers, the bike shop where Carl had worked. If I made a site visit there, perhaps a co-worker could shed some light on his personality.

I piled Rochester into the car and head south on Main Street, which eventually passed through Yardley and then hooked up with Route 13 on the far side of Morrisville. Route 13 was an industrial highway that ran along the edge of Levittown in the direction of Philadelphia, and it hadn't changed that much in the twenty-some years since my high school graduation.

For much of its distance it paralleled the rail yards, a complex system of tracks and sidings. The other side faced the back of houses in Northpark, Thornridge and Vermilion Hills. The bike shop was at the corner of Route 13 and East Penn Valley Road, not far from Pennsbury High. It was adjacent to a strip center featuring a dollar store, a  karate dojo and one of those budget insurance providers who stand a sign twirler out on the highway to bring in traffic.

A couple of lines of bikes of different sizes and configurations were parked in an open yard on the side of the store, and an oval track had been paved around them, with soft-sided orange bollards separating it.

I parked and put Rochester on his leash. We threaded our way through the lines of bikes, me looking and Rochester sniffing. A young hipster guy with a goatee and a line of tattoos up and down his arms came out of the shop, wiping his hands on a rag. "Morning. Help you?"

"I'm looking for a bike with a sidecar for my dog," I said, making it up as I went along. "A guy I met named Carl said he worked here, I should come in and he'd hook me up."

"Carl doesn't work here anymore, but I can help you," he said, holding out his hand "I'm Travis."

"Steve. And this is Rochester."

To his credit, Travis immediately bent down and made Rochester's acquaintance. "How big are you boy? Seventy pounds?"

"Closer to eighty," I said. "And strong."

"He's going to need a harness to keep him in place, too," Travis said. He looked around the yard. "Almost any bike can carry a sidecar. The better ones have a large displacement – 650 cc and higher – plenty of torque and a proper twin downtube frame."

He looked me over. "The best thing to do is start with a bike you like." I could see him registering me as a forty-something guy, drives a BMW, wears an expensive belt and shoes. "If money isn't a particular problem, I'd start with something new, because as time goes on parts will get harder to come by and people that know how to work on the bike will be fewer and fewer."

"That makes sense. That's what Carl told me."

"He knew his stuff," Travis admitted.

"He go to work somewhere else?"

Travis shook his head. "High side crash on I-95 a couple of months ago. Means his rear wheel locked up but the rear brake engaged, and he went up and over the handlebars and onto the pavement."

"Wow. That's tragic."

"It was pretty grim at the time," Travis said.

I leaned down and looked at the brake cable. I didn't remember anything I'd learned in California about motorcycle mechanics, but it looked pretty easy to fiddle with the cable. Sand down a couple of the chains, for example, so that eventually the repetitive use and pressure would cause a link to bust open.

Rochester flopped down on his butt, then stretched his paws out in front of him so he was watching both of us. "That's very unusual with a bike these days, so nothing for you to worry about," Travis reassured me. "The newer models have a lot of safety features to prevent that."

"But Carl's was an older bike?"

"He'd customized it so I can't say what was going on back there. Carl knew his shit, but realigning the brake cable or interfering with the wheel could have done anything."

He smiled grimly. "But now, let's look at a bike for you."

That was all I got out of him about Carl or his accident. Instead, he walked me over a few feet, Rochester following, and put me on a Star Bolt made by a Yamaha subsidiary. My dog sat on his haunches watching me as I gripped the handlebars. I had to admit it felt great.

As I sat there, getting a feel for the bike under me, I wondered if Peggy could have screwed with the brake cable on Carl's bike. She was a smart woman, so she could have researched vulnerabilities.

He showed me the clutch and brakes and reminded me how to shift gears. "You'll notice this is a cruiser seat," Travis said, startling me from my suspicions. "Designed for long rides, not breakneck speeds. Perfect for cruising around the countryside or a pretty day. You live in Yardley?"

"Stewart's Crossing," I said, and I was again impressed by his ability to read me as a higher-end suburbanite rather than your typical Levittown resident.

But thoughts of Carl kept popping up. If it was so easy to sabotage the bike, then anyone could have done it – another one of the Angels? A disgruntled neighbor or someone Carl had cheated?

"Great riding out that way," Travis said, once again drawing me back to the present. "Up the river road, into the hills beyond Leighville."

"I work up that way," I said. "It would be a great commuter vehicle, wouldn't it?"

"Sure would. It's light and easy to handle, and you get plenty of power from the 942-cc air-cooled engine. It's small compared with some of today's big, beefy cruisers, but overall it's a good motorcycle and a really good deal."

I'd been thinking about replacing the BMW as it got older, but I hadn't considered a motorcycle until that day. "I'd have to square it with my girlfriend," I said. "I didn't bring her today because I didn't want her to ask how I knew Carl."

"Titty bar, right?" Travis said. "Carl was great at talking to people at those places." He looked at me again. "So listen, you ready to go for a test drive before I write you up?" He nodded toward the oval track.

"Love to. But let me tie Rochester up first. I don't know how he's going to react, and I want to get a feel for the bike before I take him out."

I got off the bike, and picked up Rochester's leash. I walked him over to a light pole and tied him up there. When I got back to the bike, Travis swiped my driver's license in a gadget he held, then handed it to me to sign. "Typical insurance waiver," he said. "You agree that you're familiar enough with the bike to operate it safely, and that you hold us harmless for any injuries you incur."

I was already half in love with the idea of getting a bike so I signed eagerly. Then Travis walked over to the track and moved aside one of the soft-sided bollards. I got back on the bike and idled it over to the entrance.

Travis said, "Take it easy for the first couple or circuits, okay?"

I strapped on the helmet and gave him a thumbs up. Across from me I saw Rochester sprawled on the ground, watching me intently.

I went pretty slow the first time around, getting back my sense memory of what it had felt like back in California. Then I revved the engine and moved faster, intent on maintaining my balance, focusing on the turns. It was amazing, as if I was flying.

I did four circuits and my legs started to ache from the unaccustomed pressure, so I pulled up where Travis stood. He moved the bollard for me again, and I slid the bike back into its space.

"That was awesome," I said, as I unhooked the helmet.

"You ready to get the decision moving?"

"Like I said, I need to check with the lady. But I'll be back."

He held up a slick iPhone. "We can call her today."

I shook my head. "Need to do a little prep work before I spring it on her."

Travis lost interest in me then, and walked back into the shop. I retrieved Rochester, and he and I walked around for a few more minutes, looking at the bikes.

Rochester sniffed at a pink scrunchie on the ground—something only a woman would have worn. That reminded me of Peggy. The newspapers had said she had motive, means and opportunity in Carl's death. I understood the means and the opportunity, but what was her motive? Had she been abused, as that anonymous source suggested?

To inherit? From the look of the house on Bark Drive, it didn't appear that Carl was that wealthy, and the best job he'd had was as a supervisor at the steel mill, which he'd lost when the mill shut down.

I looked at the scrunchie again. Jealousy? Maybe Carl was having an affair and that made Peggy angry. It went against what Hunter had asked me to do, but I wanted to examine Peggy's motives in case she really was guilty.

Hunter had asked me to come up with reasonable

doubt, but I was determined to go beyond that and find out who killed Carl. That meant I needed to start sniffing out suspects.

And I had to remember that the killer might be someone completely unknown, hired by someone in Carl's life to take him out.

I realized I was spinning off onto a tangent, but I added a note to check more carefully through Carl's address book, looking for anyone who could have had access to Carl's bike, male or female.

When we got home, I took Rochester for a quick pee, then tackled the deleted messages from Carl's account. There had to be a reason why he'd suddenly trashed them all, just before his death, and I was determined to figure that out.

There were nearly a thousand of them, and for a moment I felt overwhelmed. Then my old habits kicked in and I began to organize them. I sorted them by sender first, deleting all the ones that promised to give him firmer erections or secured credit cards. That got rid of almost half the messages. Hallelujah. I only had 542 messages to work with after that.

I began copying the emails I wanted to look at further into individual folders. That way I could look at only a few at a time. The routine copying and pasting put me into a Zen state, and I was startled when a photo popped into the preview screen, definitely one that was not suitable for work.

A big-busted blonde sat naked on a Harley-Davidson chopper. Her left hand gripped the handlebar, while her right hand was down at her crotch—either hiding something or fondling herself, I couldn't tell which. I couldn't tell, however, if she was an Angel's girlfriend, or if the picture was simply one that was passed around among bikers.

I quickly skipped to the next photo, feeling a bit guilty. The rest of the images attached to that email were G-rated, photos of the male Angels with women behind them on their bikes. Could Carl have been cheating on Peggy? Would his mistress have had the same access to his bike? How could I bring that question up to Peggy?

I moved those photos to another folder, and made a note to use Google's image search to see if I could identify anyone in them. And I renamed the photo of the naked woman with an NSFW warning. God forbid I accidentally open that while meaning to show photos to Hunter Thirkell—or worse, Lili.

I managed to get about twenty-five percent moved before Lili came home from her photography expedition.

I stood up and kissed her on the cheek, glad that I hadn't stumbled on any more pornographic photos. "Have fun?" I asked.

"Hard to define," she said. "It's a lot of work learning how to operate a new camera, especially if you're accustomed to doing things a certain way. It was interesting and challenging to get it to perform the way I wanted, and to see the other things it could do." She shrugged. "I guess you could say it was fun. How about you? What did you do this morning?"

I told her about the work I was doing on Carl's emails, reinforcing that it was all legitimate. "And Rochester and I took a ride over to Levittown, to the bike shop where Carl worked."

She raised her eyebrows. "Discover anything?"

"I talked to a guy Carl worked with, and got insight into what might have caused his accident. But there was something more."

"Yes?"

"How would you feel about me getting a motorcycle license? Maybe buying a bike with a sidecar for Rochester?"

To her credit, she didn't look at me like I was crazy as I told her about my experience in California. "I only had a learner's permit there, so I'd have to get a new permit here in Pennsylvania."

"Is this some kind of midlife crisis?" she asked. "Or is

this about that woman, Peggy?"

"A little of both," I admitted. "I'm intrigued by Peggy, and how she went from the girl I knew to the woman she is today. We both hit some bad roadblocks, but I bounced back while she didn't. I'd like to think about my own resiliency."

I smiled. "I also want to understand these motorcycle guys, and I'm hoping that if I approach them as a fellow biker I'll get more information from them. And I liked riding the few times I did it. It might be fun to commute up to Friar Lake with Rochester on days when the weather is good."

"Assuming you can get a helmet for him." She cocker head had at me. "You wouldn't expect me to become some kind of biker chick, though? I'm not interested in leather jackets or tattoos."

I laughed. "You already have a leather jacket, sweetheart. That brown suede one you bought in Italy."

"Hardly biker wear." She smiled. "I trust you, Steve. If you want to get a learner's permit for a bike, you don't need my permission. And I know that if you have Rochester with you you'll be extra careful."

For a moment I remembered a similar conversation with Mary. She hadn't said that she trusted me. She had merely shrugged and said, "If you want."

I liked Lili's response better.

# 8 – About Me

Lili went upstairs to review all the images she had taken, and I turned back to Carl Landsea's emails. More sorting, deleting and filing, until a message jumped out at me with a zip file attached to it. The only words in the message were "Here it is."

I knew that kind of careful obfuscation. If you were sending something illicit, you didn't want the message to indicate that.

The message was from another one of the Angels, a guy whose email address was LoveMySled28. I knew that sled was a hipster slang for motorcycle, so that probably put the sender a decade younger than Carl.

When I tried to open it, though, the zip file had been password protected. "Oh, come on," I said. "Another password to crack? Really?" I was frustrated—it seemed like every time I found a lead, some kind of obstacle popped up.

Rochester got up and walked over to me. I stroked his head as I looked at the unzip screen where I was asked for the password. How in the world was I going to figure that out, when I knew nothing about the person who had sent it?

I exited the zip program and went looking for other messages from LoveMySled28 Maybe he had sent the password in a separate message.

No luck.

Rochester licked my hand, and I felt reassured. It was as if he was saying, "You can do this, Daddy."

There are two ways you can encrypt and password-protect a zip file. The first, nicknamed Zip Crypto, was relatively easy to crack. All you needed was a password generator program, as I had. The second method, AES-256, was a lot harder – almost impossible to crack.

I checked the header text for the file, and gods be praised, LoveMySled28 had simply used Zip Crypto. That meant I could crack the password, though it might take a lot of time. I was also able to look at the contents of the zip folder, which wasn't helpful – it was an Excel spreadsheet called *numbers.xls*. Could have been any kind of numbers – like the phone numbers for group members.

This time, because I didn't have any personal information to include, I chose a different password cracking tool. This one used several techniques, including the simplest, trying passwords from a dictionary. It could also perform a rainbow table attack, using a precomputed table for reversing the encryption used on passwords. And finally, if all else failed, it could carry brute-force attacks by slamming the zip file with an onslaught of password options. It also had special techniques for zip file encryption.

I initiated the program and let it go. It could take hours to break into the zip file, days, who knows, maybe weeks. I had gotten so caught up in that question that I'd stopped petting Rochester, which made him fretful, and he began bothering me for a walk.

All of southeastern Pennsylvania was suffering from a heat wave, and the air felt like a big wet blanket. As an adult with a dog who needed a lot of walking, I felt the heat a lot more. Fortunately, golden retrievers have an undercoat that provides a layer of insulation for them, allowing them to feel warmer in winter and cooler in summer. Right then I wished I had a similar situation, but all I could do was sweat my way along, trying to stick to the shady side of the street. I hoped Wildwood Crest would be better—at least there would be ocean breezes.

Rochester and I went down Sarajevo Way – all the streets in River Bend are named for Eastern European cities – and once again ran into Bob Freehl in his driveway, tinkering with the motorcycle he usually kept locked up in his garage. "Nice day for a ride," I said to him. "I had a motorcycle license in California and I'm thinking of getting a bike myself."

"Nothing like it," Bob said. "As long as you wear a

helmet and observe all the safety rules."

That was Bob. Once a cop, always a cop.

"If I were you I'd rent a bike first before you buy one," he said. "Say, why don't you come on a poker run with me next weekend? Most of the money we raise goes to a cancer charity, and it would give you a chance to get your feet wet."

"What's a poker run?" I asked.

"A bunch of bikers go from one checkpoint to the next, collecting a playing card at each one. At the end, the guy with the best hand wins."

"Sounds like fun," I said, as Rochester pulled me forward to sniff something exciting. "I'll email you for the details."

After I got home and emailed Bob, he responded quickly, sending me to the website where I could register. It cost $25, and began and ended at the Willow Grove Mall, about a half hour away from us on the north side of Philadelphia. As Bob had said, I'd collect a playing card when I signed in, and then one more at each of four stops throughout the countryside. Whoever had the best hand upon the return to Willow Grove won a prize.

I checked the password software on the other laptop. Faster than I could have done it manually, it was attempting to open the zipped file, being confronted with the request for a password, entering a suggestion and getting rejected, then starting the whole process over again. It was almost mesmerizing to watch, but I forced myself to return to my regular laptop, where I switched over to the Pennsylvania DMV website.

I downloaded the application for a motorcycle learner's permit and a PDF of the motorcycle operator's manual. As I did, Rochester rested his head on my knee, and I couldn't tell if he approved of what I was doing, if he didn't — or if he just wanted attention. The only one of those choices I could do anything about was the third one, so I scratched behind his ears and told him what a good boy he was, and he opened his mouth in a big doggy grin.

By the time Lili came back downstairs, I was sitting on the sofa reading the electronic version of the manual on my iPad, with Rochester taking up a big chunk of real estate beside me. He scrambled off at her approach and settled on the floor as she slid in beside me. "What are you reading?"

I showed her the screen. "You're really doing this," she said. "Getting a motorcycle. When you decide on something, you move fast."

"As I did when I met you," I said. "But you're for keeps, and the motorcycle is only temporary, while I see if riding one will give me any insights into Peggy Doyle and

Carl Landsea. I'm just applying for my learner's permit and then renting a bike."

I told her about the poker run. "I'll be with Bob Freehl the whole time in case I get into any trouble."

She snorted. "You? Get into trouble?" She stood up. "You keep reading. I'll get some dinner going. How would you feel about a big salad and the leftover eggplant parmigiana?"

"I'd feel delighted."

My interest in biking rose as I read through the handbook. It was interesting to learn that a driver shouldn't assumed that a motorcycle was turning just because its turn signal was flashing. A bike's turn signals might not turn off automatically, like a vehicle's.

I hadn't realized that most motorcycle/vehicle crashes happened at intersections, where a vehicle turned left in front of a moving bike or moped, when the driver of the vehicle should have yielded the right of way. I'd have to be particularly careful of that.

I took notes as I read, so that I'd remember the material when I had to take the online exam.

When Lili had the salad and eggplant prepared, we sat together at the kitchen table and ate, talking about the photographs she'd taken that day and the ideas she had for incorporating the new cameras into her curriculum.

After dinner, the software still hadn't found the password for the zip file from LoveMySled28 so I went back to Carl's emails, getting another fifty percent or so sorted into separate files. I kept looking back at the password cracker, and I realized that there had to be a way to automate what I was doing.

I occasionally prowled through a couple of file sharing sites on the dark web, using the Tor browser to preserve my anonymity, and I kept a decent archive of interesting programs on Caroline's old laptop. Some of them were hacker tools that allowed me to bypass security features on a web server, but many of them were basic shareware that allowed me to create or manipulate images, edit PDF files and so on.

I minimized the password window and dipped into the folder where I kept those programs, and found one that would search the content of each file for keywords I put in. I set up one search for "Levitt" and another for "Angels." At least that would give me a head start.

While I waited for that program to sort through all the emails, I turned to the leather-bound address book Peggy had given me. Carl Landsea had surprisingly good handwriting for a scum ball—almost as if he'd had some training as an architect or draftsman. The letters weren't connected, as they'd be in cursive writing, but they were neatly formed and a pleasure to look at.

His writing reminded me of that of a huge, menacing guy I knew in prison, who was there for life after killing the entire family of a man who owed him a hundred bucks. His handwriting was beautiful, and his explanation was his Catholic school upbringing. "The nuns made us write pretty," he had said.

With Carl's address book in hand, I went back to my own laptop and began using Google and my subscription site to search every name there, looking for connections to Levitt's Angels or anyone else with a motive to kill Carl. It was slow work, but I was dogged about hunting up every association I could find. I opened a Word document and began listing the names and what I could find, beginning with Martin Anderson.

From a combination of websites and emails to the Levitt's Angels, I discovered that Anderson was forty-five, a year younger than I was, married, and owned a home on Bayberry Lane in Levittown with a substantial mortgage. He was a sales rep for one of the mobile phone carriers, rode a Suzuki GSF600, and had no criminal record.

I kept going. When I got to a Levitt's Angel named Frank Diehl, I found that he four years before, he had gone to prison on drug charges. He been released about three months before Carl's death. Something about his name tickled in my brain, and I went back to the notes I'd taken about my conversation with Peggy. She had mentioned an Angel named Frank, one with a funny nickname. From the email folders, I found that his buddies called him Big Diehl.

Then I switched over to my legal offense database site and put in Frank Diehl. He had a couple of minor convictions, like Carl, but then he'd been pulled in for a pretty big sale of heroin to an undercover operator.

What jumped out was that Carl Landsea had been a co-defendant in the case that had put Diehl in prison. That was the one that resulted in Carl getting off with a fine and time served. Had Carl turned on his fellow biker to get that deal?

Could that have been a motive for Diehl to come after Landsea once he was free? Diehl had been a member of the Levitt's Angels as well, so he probably had the skill to fiddle with Carl's bike.

But why didn't Hunter come up with Diehl himself? He had access to the same legal databases I had. Maybe he had—he hadn't told me anything about his own research, after all, just that he'd been looking into the Levitt's Angels. But in case he hadn't, I gathered everything I could about him from my various databases and the deleted emails from Carl's computer.

Frank and Carl had clearly been friends; there were old messages from before Diehl's incarceration about going out together, getting drunk and looking for women. They'd compared notes on the dancers at Club Hott; while Frank agreed with Carl that Peggy was sexy, Frank preferred women with bigger booties.

Frank owned no property in his own name, but his name regularly came up in connection with that of a woman named Olga Diehl, who owned a house on Tulip Tree Road in the Twin Oaks neighborhood of Levittown. His wife, or ex? Nope, another search indicated she was eighty-one years old, so probably his mother.

I couldn't find any current work record for him, so I wasn't sure he had returned to Bucks County after his release from prison. I could have tried to hack into a government database to see where he had been assigned a parole officer— but that was far beyond what Hunter had asked me to find.

I found a bunch of messages from Frank Diehl that mentioned words like pickup and shipment and distribution. Carl and Diehl had both been arrested on a drug distribution charge, and it looked like Carl had cut a deal by testifying against his buddy. That might give Diehl a motive to exact revenge on Carl—and I knew that Diehl had been released from prison shortly before Carl's death. There were no messages between them after Diehl's release from prison, but perhaps they'd been in touch by phone.

I composed an email to Hunter, indicating exactly what steps I had taken to discover the information. When I hit send, I expected to feel satisfied — I'd done what he asked. I had found a solid suspect who could provide reasonable doubt that Peggy wasn't the only one with means, motive and opportunity to kill Carl Landsea. He could take that to the district attorney and the judge, and use it to shift attention away from Peggy.

But I didn't feel that I'd done all I could. I realized that I had fallen into the pattern I'd followed several times before. This project, as it was, had morphed from a favor to Hunter into something deeper about me and my obsession to work through a puzzle, to solve a mystery. I wanted to know who killed Carl Landsea, and why.

# 9 – Test Drives

By the time Rochester and I returned from our bedtime walk, the sorter program had put aside about two hundred fifty of Carl's formerly deleted emails that contained either the word "Levitt" or "Angel." But I was tired and Lili was waiting for me in bed, so desire trumped curiosity.

The next day was a busy one at Friar Lake, and fortunately the PennDOT office in Bensalem was closed on Monday so I didn't stress about trying to sneak away there. After dinner that evening, while Lili was upstairs fiddling with the photos she'd taken over the weekend, I began to read through the emails the search program had pulled out for me.

Most of the messages could be deleted—they contained the same kind of material that had been in the group emails I'd looked at before. Advice on bike problems, get-togethers and so on.

I was surprised to find a few from Peggy in that batch, and wondered why she'd email him rather than text him. Then I remembered that she'd said he had simple flip phone, and that he didn't text. It was sad that she had to email him to get his attention, and I hoped Lili and I would never come to that point.

In one message, Peggy complained about how much

time Carl was spending with the Angels instead of with her. In another she seemed plaintive – why did Carl want his bike between his legs instead of her? And then in a third, she seemed to be accusing Carl of being gay, wanting to spend all his time with guys instead of with his wife.

Those messages indicated there was trouble in the relationship, though I couldn't find any evidence to support what that anonymous caller had said to the cops, that Carl was beating Peggy. Instead, she sounded lonely and increasingly angry that she was being ignored.

What if Peggy was guilty, and something I did kept her from getting convicted? Suppose, as the gossips suggested, she had killed husbands one and two and gotten away with those as well?

That led me to wonder if perhaps there wasn't anything in those deleted messages that would lead to the person who killed Carl. But why had he dumped them all, just before he died? Was it just coincidence? Or had he been cleaning up something that he didn't want anyone else to know about?

* * *

The next afternoon I was able to get out of Friar Lake early and I took a quick run down I-95 to the PennDOT office in Bensalem, where I picked up my learner's permit. Rochester wasn't happy he had to stay in the car, but I parked in the shade and left the windows cracked. By the time I returned he had that mournful look on his face intended to guilt me into a biscuit—but it was his bad luck I didn't have any in the car.

On my way home I called Rick. "You busy later?"

"You want to meet at the Drunken Hessian?" he asked. "I could use a break. Been a rough time at the station."

"If you can give me a ride into Tullytown, then I'll treat you to a beer and a burger." I explained that I wanted to rent a motorcycle so I could go on the poker run with Bob Freehl that Sunday.

"A motorcycle? What brought this on?"

"I'll explain on the way."

I took Rochester home, fed and walked him, and told Lili I was going out with Rick to pick up the bike. "Have fun," she said. "I just got a new e-book of photos by Gregory Crewdson and I want to immerse myself in his images."

Rick picked me up about a half hour later, and on the way to Pennsy Choppers he grilled me about the connection between my new interest in biking and Peggy Doyle's case.

"It's not exactly a new interest," I protested. "I had a learner's permit in California. If it hadn't been for everything that happened after I hacked those credit sites, I might have bought a bike back then."

"But right now you're just doing this because your old gal pal needs help," he said.

"At least I'm not hacking," I said.

"There's that. You say you're going to do this ride with Freehl?"

"He'll look out for me. It'll be almost like having you there."

"Yeah, me when I'm thirty years older and retired from the force."

"He's still a pretty sharp guy. And he knows about bikes."

"At least you're not hacking," Rick echoed as he pulled into the parking lot.

Rick followed me into the store, where we found Travis on his back on the showroom floor as he tinkered with the chain on a bright red moped. He looked tired and frustrated, and there was a spot of oil on his goatee.

"I'm kind of surprised you came back," he said, as he stood up. He wiped his greasy hands on a blue bandana. "A lot of guys your age come in to look around but never follow through."

I bristled at the "guys your age" comment, especially because I noticed Rick smirking. But hell, I was in my mid-forties, prime time for a midlife crisis, so I couldn't blame

Travis for making the assumption.

"I'd like to rent a bike for a couple of weeks before I make a final decision," I said. "One with a sidecar for the dog."

"I've got a used Honda I can let you have," he said. "It's a pretty popular model, and though it's got about 75,000 miles on it, I just worked it over last week."

I agreed to take it. While Rick browsed around the store, Travis made a copy of my driver's license and the Pennsylvania learner's permit I'd picked up at the PennDOT office. Then he found a helmet for Rochester and a harness I could use to strap him in place. The last thing I wanted was the big dog to jump out of the sidecar.

While Travis put the bike and the sidecar together, I walked over to Rick. "You ever want to ride a motorcycle?" I asked.

He shook his head. "Seen too many dumb bikers who end up in the hospital or the morgue," he said.

"You can be a careful biker," I said. "And it's pretty cool when you're out on the road, kind of like flying."

"I'll stick to the ski slopes if I want that kind of experience."

It was funny to think of myself as more adventurous than Rick — I was the dull administrator who faced nothing more dangerous on a daily basis than the possibility of slipping and falling while walking Rochester. Rick had taken down angry drunks, disarmed would-be robbers, and dealt with violent domestic incidents. But maybe that was the point; he got all the thrills he needed at work.

When we saw that Travis had the bike ready, Rick and I walked outside, and he said, "I'll follow you to the Drunken Hessian. Try not to cause an accident, all right?"

"I'll do my best."

I was grateful for the long summer day, because it was still daylight as I navigated my way back down Route 13, and I remembered how much I'd enjoyed that brief time back in California when I had the bike, before my old life fell apart.

I had a good new one, I reminded myself. And I needed to pay attention to the road, not wallow in the past. I resisted the urge to dart around slower drivers, leaning back with my hands firmly on the handlebars, and let the scenery roll past me. Then a long stretch opened up ahead of me, and I revved the engine and zoomed forward, the hot summer air rushing past me, my shirt ballooning out behind me. I'd take this over skiing any day.

I had to slow down once I turned off Route 13 and onto Main Street in Morrisville. Every half mile a car or truck was slowing to turn or changing lanes abruptly. By the time I pulled into the parking lot at the Drunken Hessian, my arms were shaky and my back had cramped.

I pulled my helmet off as Rick came up to me. "You handled the bike pretty well." Then he smiled. "That is, after you ran over the curb outside the bike shop."

I ignored the jibe. "I had to concentrate," I admitted. "But I liked it. I'll see how the poker run goes with Bob Freehl before I make any permanent decisions, though."

We went inside, ordered a couple of beers and our favorite burgers. I always got the General Lafayette, with ham and swiss over a medium-rare patty, and my mouth was watering as I ordered it.

Rick looked so neat, with his short hair perfectly in place, that I kept trying to smooth down my own helmet hair. "So, Levitt's Angels," he said, after the waitress had delivered our bottles and we'd declined to have them poured out into glasses. "I did some research."

"And?"

"I've changed my opinion as I read more closely. They're not a bunch of doctors and lawyers riding Harleys, but they're also not as bad as people might think. The younger ones have at least some college under their belt—one of the guys I read about even took police science courses at Liberty Bell University, aiming to be a motorcycle cop."

I'd seen the billboards for that for-profit college, which asked students to "strike a bell for freedom of education at Liberty Bell U."

Rick picked a piece of lint from the sleeve of his neatly pressed plaid shirt. I knew that he had his shirts laundered at the Wash 'n Go around the corner from the Drunken Hessian, and his slacks pressed there, too.

"There are a couple of rotten apples, sure," he continued. "But you find that almost anywhere."

"Let me guess. Big Diehl?"

He nodded. "He's one of a couple, along with Carl Landsea, who have records."

"Carl gave up Diehl in exchange for a lighter sentence, giving Diehl a motive to kill Carl, now that he's out of prison."

"If you know all this stuff already what do you need me for?"

"I value your insights," I said, my tongue only partly in my cheek.

Rick snorted. "I spoke to a guy on the FBI's gang task force, and he said the Levitt's Angels are small potatoes to them, though they have some connections to drug dealing and prostitution. Nothing we didn't already know, or surmise."

"I want to go back to Big Diehl," I said. "Do you think he has a credible motive for killing Carl Landsea?"

Rick shrugged. "Not for me to say. Yeah, he could have held onto his anger at Carl and gone after him as soon as he got out of prison. But all the interviews I read with him in the police files paint a guy who was always looking for the next big scheme—more a dreamer than a killer."

"Prison can change you," I said. "It can make you harder if you let it. Or you can recognize you have a new chance when you get out and focus on taking advantage of that."

"It looks like his new chance isn't panning out that well," Rick said. "His PO told me that he's living with his mother in Levittown. She has Alzheimer's and Diehl's looking after her."

That must be the Olga Diehl I'd discovered. I had very mixed feelings about that. On the one hand, I could imagine it was tough for a biker dude like Big Diehl to come out of prison only to end up taking care of a mother with dementia. But on the other hand, I missed my own parents and was sorry I hadn't had the chance to look after them when they needed me.

I realized that if Diehl had indeed turned over a new leaf and was focused on taking care of his mother, that left Hunter without a credible alternative suspect to Peggy. I was glad that I hadn't stopped searching after sending him the email about Diehl.

"Any other Angels who might have had a beef with Carl?" I asked.

"Not that I found in the case records. But of course that was mostly about Diehl, not about Landsea."

I felt like a balloon that had been punctured. I was back to square one trying to help Peggy, and my shore vacation with Lili was coming up quickly. I needed to focus on the positive of that trip, though, not the deadline that it pushed forward.

"I am so looking forward to Wildwood Crest," I said. "Have to keep Rochester out of the ocean, though. I don't want to spend my whole vacation shampooing salt water out of his coat."

"Tamsen wants to get out of the heat, so we might go up to Canada for a week. Still in the planning stages, though. We have to introduce the idea to Justin, and work out the schedules with her sister and make sure Justin can stay with them. Probably take Rascal with us, but if not I'll check with you and see if you and Lili can keep him."

I restricted myself to only one beer so that I'd be clear-headed to ride the bike home, and Rick did the same. It was dark by the time we left the Drunken Hessian, but I knew those local streets by heart and made my way back to River

Bend without incident.

Lili was sitting up in bed with her iPad, reading the photo book, when I came in. "How was your first bike ride?"

"Pretty good." I repeated what I had told Rick, that I wasn't going to make any decisions until after the poker run with Bob on Sunday.

"You think I could take a test ride with you one day?" she asked. "I used to have a Ducati scooter when I lived in Italy but I've never been on a big bike."

"That would be awesome."

It rained the next morning, which was frustrating because I wanted to test out the bike some more. And even more joy – I received a notice from the human resources department that I had twelve online course modules to complete, on everything from sexual harassment to firearms on campus to new issues in financial aid.

I watched the first three videos and took the corresponding quizzes. Then I switched over to the thousand and one details I had to handle before the arrival of a group of incoming freshman for STEM workshops in early August. When lunchtime rolled around, it was still rainy, so I ate my sandwich at my desk. I gave Rochester a couple of pieces of turkey, and then he rolled onto his side for a nap.

I sat there staring out the big glass window at the trees.

If Frank Diehl didn't kill Carl Landsea, and I was assuming that Peggy didn't either, then who did? One of the Angels? Someone else? How would I figure that out?

Rochester rose and came over to me, nudging my arm to see if I had any more turkey to give him. I hit the computer mouse with my elbow, and it woke up my computer, which was open to my email screen.

I remembered that I hadn't finished going through the deleted emails, and I resolved to do that at home. "Thanks, boy," I said, as I ruffled his ears. "I appreciate the help. But I still don't have any more turkey to give you."

He yawned and slumped to the floor again. But remembering the emails I had to look through energized me. Maybe there'd be a new clue in one of those.

# 10 – Another Old Friend

I couldn't get back to the deleted emails until after we'd had dinner that evening, and I'd given Rochester his post-prandial walk. I made it a short one, though, because it was still drizzling, the streets damp and littered with wet leaves.

I went through each of the messages that had mentioned Levitt's Angels, and I was surprised to find Phil Prior on the list, and to discover from that for a while he had dated a girl I knew in high school.

Elise Lewis sat next to me in homeroom for two years, where we were placed alphabetically. We had joked at the time that no one could come between us — Levitan and Lewis. Since then she'd married and divorced and gone back to her maiden name. We had become Facebook friends a couple of years before.

I logged in there, and looked her up. She was a stylist at a hair salon in Levittown, and most of her posts were pictures of hair styles, either those of celebrities or ones she had cut. She liked the same kind of music we had in high school, Bruce Springsteen and Southside Johnny and the Asbury Jukes, and her movie favorites were all romantic comedies.

I sent her a message asking if we could get together some time. I didn't want to tip my hand about the Angels or

Peggy Doyle, so I simply said I was eager to catch up with folks I had known back in high school.

I spent a few minutes scanning through recent posts, then switched over to my hacker group to see if I'd gotten any responses to my question about the curious thrill I got logging into Carl's email account, even though I had legitimate reasons for being there.

MamaHack, a wife and mother who was about my age, had responded the night before. "I still feel weird when I have to log into my kids' schools to check their grades or sign permissions," she wrote. "Even though it's perfectly legitimate for me to be there. I guess this is something that's gotten wired into our brains."

She closed with "DON'T DO ANYTHING WRONG!!" in all caps, followed by a couple of heart emojis.

I sent her a brief thanks, and added that I was doing my best to stick to the straight and narrow, though I added that it was hard when there was so much temptation around.

As I finished, a message popped up from Elise Lewis. "I have to work tomorrow evening but the salon's dead slow after six," she wrote. "Want to come by? We have a Keurig machine in the back."

I made sure to mention Lili in my response, so that Elise wouldn't think I was flirting. "My girlfriend says I'm looking kind of shaggy, so slot me in for a cut at six-thirty. We can talk while you make me handsome."

She responded a little later with "LOL, I'll do my best."

By bedtime, the rain had stopped, though branches still dripped on me as I took Rochester for his last walk of the day. Had hacking gotten wired into my brain, I wondered, as we walked, stopped, and walked again. I already knew that I had to be vigilant around my use of those hacking tools to be sure I never stepped over the legal line. But had something happened to my brain so that even legitimate work triggered those old impulses?

The next morning dawned sparkly and fresh. Rochester demonstrated that he wasn't eager to hop into the sidecar by planting his front paws on the driveway and lowering his head. I pulled a treat out of my pocket and waved it in front of him, and he looked up.

I tugged a bit on his leash, and he looked up, at the treat in my hand and then at me. He sat up and put his front paws on the sidecar, and I helped him up and into the seat. I gave him the treat then, and he chewed it noisily while I strapped him into the harness.

Travis had said that as long as I had him strapped in and drove carefully, I didn't need a helmet for him. "They're mostly for dogs who ride pillion," he said. "If he gets comfortable enough with the bike that he can ride on the seat behind you, come back and we'll custom-order a helmet for him."

Rochester strained against the harness and whimpered, and I scratched behind his ears and told him he was a good boy. Then I sat on the bike and turned on the engine, and he crouched low on the seat.

"Maybe this isn't a good idea, boy," I said. He looked up at me with a mournful expression.

"I tell you what, let's try a few miles, and if you really don't like it we'll come home."

He looked down at the floor, and I blew out a breath. "Nothing ventured, nothing gained," I said, and I backed the bike carefully out of the driveway. I drove slowly through River Bend, getting a feel for the way the bike shifted with the dog in the sidecar. I couldn't take curves as quickly as I might have, and the speed bumps throughout the community were a particular problem.

By the time we'd traveled a few miles up River Road, I felt comfortable with the bike, and gradually Rochester got accustomed to the ride. He sat up on the seat, as much as he could with the restraints, and sniffed the air with his long snout. Whenever I could I reached over to pet him. I was relieved that he enjoyed the ride, and I relaxed and enjoyed the warm breeze at it rushed past me, bringing with it the funky smell of the river, mixed with automobile exhaust and fertilizer. Not the best combination, but it was exhilarating, even better than riding in a convertible with the top down.

By the time we reached Friar Lake, Rochester was a motorcycle convert. He didn't even want to jump out of the sidecar, as if he thought he could convince me to keep on driving.

I spent a chunk of the day completing more of those online programs, including one on first time in college students, another on student privacy, and a third on financial aid. Because aid fraud cost the government nearly $200 million dollars a year, Eastern had to institute new measures to track the reasons for class failure, and we had to add an indicator on our grade roll that identified whether a student who failed had done so because of lack of attendance, or just poor performance.

I remembered that Rick had mentioned at least one of the Levitt's Angels had gone to college at Liberty Bell University, one of the for-profit colleges that had sprung up in the last couple of years in the Philadelphia suburbs like mushrooms after a spring rain. I applauded anyone who wanted to better him or herself through education, but from what I'd read, colleges like LBU were more concerned with collecting tuition than providing education.

But maybe I was just a snob with an education from a very good small college, as Eastern billed itself.

When it was time to leave Friar Lake, Rochester hopped eagerly into the sidecar. It was windy along the river, and I had to clutch tightly to the handlebars to keep the bike from wavering. It was tougher than I remembered from riding in California – but I was also ten years older, and I needed to give myself time to get back in the groove of riding.

Lili and I ate an early dinner and I told her I was heading out for a haircut. "You don't need a barber," I said to Rochester, when he wanted to come with me. "You take care of getting rid of excess hair yourself."

"Which reminds me," Lili said. "Somebody ought to vacuum up the dog hair soon."

"I can do that when I get back." I kissed her cheek and body-blocked Rochester from following me out the front door.

I'd had enough of biking for the day so I drove the BMW out to Levittown. The Curl Up and Dye Salon was located in a strip shopping center near the Oxford Valley Mall, sandwiched between an emergency medical clinic and a comic book store.

I recognized Elise Lewis right away, more from her Facebook pictures than any long-ago memories. Her hair was probably a shade or two blacker than natural, and her eyes were rimmed with black mascara. "Steve!" she squealed when I walked in. "Wow. Long time no see."

We hugged. "We always said nothing would come between us," she reminded me. "Except maybe twenty years or so."

"You look good, Elise," I said, when we pulled apart. "You've been here in Levittown since we graduated?"

"I married a Marine," she said. "We moved around for a while. South Carolina, Germany, California, Okinawa. But I always knew I wanted to come back home."

"And you did."

She nodded. "Come on, sit in the chair and I'll tell you whole sordid story."

She kept talking as she wrapped the cape around my shoulders. "Shane was always a controlling bastard, but for the longest time I thought it was the Marines who were making him act that way. We were in foreign countries, so of course he was concerned about my safety, who I went out with, where I went."

She grabbed her clippers. "Anything special you want?"

I shrugged. "Work your magic."

"When we got back to the States it only got worse. He

had to know the passwords for my email and my Facebook, and if he didn't like something I posted, he'd delete it. We fought more and more, and finally I walked out."

She began buzzing the back of my head with her clippers. "My dad died around that time, and the divorce took a long time, so I moved back in with my mom for a while and went to beauty school."

"Sorry to hear about your dad," I said. "I guess we've been on kind of parallel paths."

I told her about Mary's miscarriages, my hacking, and our divorce. "My dad died while I was in prison, so I moved into the townhouse he bought in Stewart's Crossing after my mom died."

"Getting old sucks, doesn't it?" Elise said, as she tilted my head down. "You keep losing people you love."

"At least I found someone new," I said. I told her briefly about Lili. "How about you?"

"After my divorce, my self-confidence was in the toilet," she said. "I dated a couple of guys, then landed on this one guy, Phil. He treated me like a queen—flowers and jewelry and dinners out." She shrugged. "But eventually I realized he was just the same as Shane, just showed the control stuff differently."

I remembered Professor del Presto's comments about

choosing someone who would make us change in the way we knew we had to. How many times would that have to happen before we could break our bad patterns?

She started snipping stray hairs. "He was a biker, and he kept calling me his lady, taking me out with this group of guys he hung around with to show me off like I was a thing, not a person."

"A group of bikers?" I asked, grateful she'd finally given me the opportunity to shift the conversation toward what I wanted to know. "Not the Levitt's Angels?"

"How do you know about them?"

I had to wait until she'd finished trimming my eyebrows to answer. "A friend of mine from high school dated one of them. Peggy Doyle. Or Peggy Landsea, now."

She stopped in mid-trim of my right sideburn. "Get out of here. You know Peggy?"

"Sure, long time. We went on the summer study program in France together."

"Small frigging world, isn't it? I have to say, Peggy was such a quiet, mousy kind of girl I was stunned she had the balls to kill Carl."

"You think she did it?"

She began trimming again. "Isn't that what the police say?"

"Yeah, but I'm not sure. Like you said, she doesn't have the personality to kill somebody."

"We all can do things we never think we can," Elise said darkly. "You keep an animal in a cage long enough, it'll do anything to break out."

"Carl kept a short leash on Peggy?"

"Carl was a lot like Shane and Phil," Elise said. "Always covering up the control shit with sweet words." She stepped back and motioned me to look in the mirror. "And Phil told me that Carl was a real horndog. He was having an affair for at least part of the time he and Peggy were married."

"Another biker's girl?"

She shook her head. "Phil would never tell me her name, but he said I'd be surprised if I knew the kind of woman she was." She pulled off the cape and shook it out. "I took that to mean she was either prettier than I'd expect, or smarter."

I thanked Elise and tried to pay her, but she said the cut was on her, because she was so glad to reconnect with me. I stuck a twenty in the tip jar when she wasn't looking.

So Carl was cheating on Peggy, and with an unexpected woman. Unexpected in what way?

# 11 – Passion

The entrance gate to River Bend was broken when I got home, so I had to take out my wallet and show my driver's license to the guard in order to get in. I dropped my wallet on the seat, and when I carried it into the house I left it on the dining room table.

Rochester, of course, was all over me, so excited to see me after I'd abandoned him for an hour. I trekked upstairs, Rochester dogging me, and found Lili reading in the bedroom. She liked my haircut, and after I shucked my shoes and my shirt and emptied my pockets into the jewelry box on the nightstand, I left her there and went back downstairs to look at the password cracker program.

For a moment I didn't realize what I was looking at — why wasn't the screen zipping through possible passwords? Then I realized the software had finally been able to open up the zip file that LoveMySled28 had sent Carl, and I was looking at the unzipped contents of the file.

All I got, though, was a single Excel spreadsheet of nearly 200 nine-digit numbers. At first I thought they might be phone numbers, so I arranged them in numerical order, looking for recognizable area codes. But then I realized that my own phone number, with area code, exchange and number, was ten digits, not nine.

Credit card numbers? I thought they had to be longer than nine digits, and I did a quick check with a site that would tell you if a credit card number was authentic, based on its ability to pass a series of tests called the Luhn algorithm. It wasn't something you wanted to bother with yourself, but if, for example, you were accepting credit card numbers online, you'd want to be sure the number you were given was a valid one before completing the transaction.

The numbers I had couldn't be credit card numbers, because they weren't long enough – those had to be sixteen to nineteen digits long in order for the Luhn algorithm to work. But if they weren't card numbers, what were they?

I was staring at the screen mindlessly when I heard Rochester licking something. He'd had a hotspot a couple of months before, so I was alert to the sound of his tongue working over some place or thing. "What are you up to, boy?" I asked, as I looked up.

He had my wallet between his paws, and several of my credit cards had spilled out. "Oh, Rochester!" I said. "That is not yours."

I reached over and took the wallet from him, then scooped up the cards from the floor. One of them was my social security card, which I'd had laminated years before to protect it.

I'd long since memorized the number. All nine digits of it, I realized. Like the numbers on the screen.

"Rochester, you're a genius!" I jumped up and got him a dental treat, and while he chewed on it I looked at those numbers. If I reformatted them to include dashes after the first three letters, then the next two, they looked just like Social Security numbers.

I found another site, this one that would validate SSNs. I typed in the first number, and a results screen popped up. According to Social Security Administration data, this SSN had been issued in Pennsylvania sometime between 1966 and 1967. It did not appear in the SSA Death Masterfile, which indicated it was still valid.

I tried a couple of other random numbers from the file, and got back similar results.

Somehow, LoveMySled28 had gotten hold of nearly two hundred social security numbers, and forwarded them to Carl Landsea. But what was Carl supposed to do with them? Sell them to illegal aliens?

He didn't work in yard maintenance or house cleaning, where he might meet illegal aliens, and I found it hard to imagine Carl sitting around at a titty bar asking guys if they wanted to buy social security numbers.

There were a lot of things you could do with someone's social security number. Use it and a birthday to get a driver's license, a bank account, establish a credit card, and so on. But all of that was relatively sophisticated, and I didn't see Carl as the kind of guy who could handle a big scheme like that.

Friday morning I called Hunter and verified that he'd received my email about Frank Diehl. Even though I didn't feel that strongly about Diehl as a suspect anymore, I wanted to follow up. "Peggy told me that he's the one Angel she thinks could have killed Carl."

"I looked over what you sent, and I reached out to the prosecutor to ask him what he thinks."

"I found something else." I explained about the file of Social Security numbers that Carl had received by email.

"I don't see how they can provide reasonable doubt that someone other than Peggy killed Carl unless you can find out more about what Carl was supposed to do with them," Hunter said. "You know anything about the guy who sent them?"

"Just his email address. But I can keep digging."

"You do that, and keep me in the loop."

I had some free time at Friar Lake that afternoon since the volume of college emails dropped off dramatically on Friday afternoons. I had no programs set up the following week, and Lili and I were planning to leave for Wildwood Crest in a week, so I wasn't going to start anything big.

I spent a few hours looking online at all the things you could do with a stolen Social Security number. The Social Security Administration warned that a thief could use your number to establish credit cards or loans without your knowledge and leave you on the hook for big bills.

Another site warned that a thief could access your Social Security or unemployment benefits. They could quickly drain those resources, preventing you from collecting those funds when you need them. A thief could also file a fraudulent tax return in your name, claiming your refund. I knew a lot of people who waited until the very last minute to file their returns—giving thieves a couple of months to file a return before the legit person had a chance to. Even if you weren't due a refund, the crooks could manipulate your data to make it look like you deserved one, and take it.

Someone could also use your information to initiate costly medical treatment, then leave you on the hook for deductibles and co-pays. I read an article about an ordinary guy who had worked for a while in a doctor's office. He was a daydreamer with a passionate desire to live on an island in the South Pacific, surrounded by sexy women serving him tropical drinks. He stole Social Security numbers from patients and used their information to fill hundreds of prescriptions for opioids and other pain relievers, then sold them on the black market. He was just about to board a flight for Tahiti when the FBI arrested him.

He'd confessed to having tunnel vision – focused so hard on achieving his goal that he ignored the moral and legal implications of what he was doing. He was following his passion, he said.

What kind of passion had caused someone to kill Carl Landsea? Elise Lewis had said that Carl was controlling. Peggy's emails to Carl had a desperate tone—could she have been so caught up in wanting him to love her that when he didn't, she killed him?

It could have been the same kind of tunnel vision that the Tahiti-bound office manager had experienced. When Mary suffered her second miscarriage, I could have hugged her, told her how much I loved her, and talked about ways we could both heal without going back into debt. But instead I got the idea of flagging her credit reports, and that's all I focused on.

I realized only later that the reason why I'd focused on that credit bureau option was because I didn't love Mary enough to overcome all that had come between us—and I knew in my heart she didn't love me enough, either. But instead of facing that pain, I'd turned to hacking.

I never would have hurt Mary, but I could see how someone like Peggy, with fewer options, could have turned to the idea of killing Carl. Especially if she knew enough about his motorcycle to be able to fiddle with the brake chain. That was a lot more passive than attacking him with a knife, for example. And Peggy was smart enough to know that if she was careful, no one might connect her with the accident.

Then the newspaper reporter had discovered the deaths of her two previous husbands, and she'd been pilloried in the media and all but convicted there, even though she'd never been charged in either of the first two deaths.

Once again I worried that Peggy had killed Carl, and that if I was successful in helping Hunter establish reasonable doubt, I might be contributing to letting a murdered go free.

I kept churning through those issues as I drove home from work, walked Rochester, and sat down to dinner with Lili. She'd made a big salad of Romaine lettuce tossed with chunks of rotisserie chicken, cherry tomatoes from the farmer's market, and Caesar dressing.

I looked up from the bowl in front of me. "You know I love you, don't you?"

She put down her fork and looked over at me. One of her auburn curls had come loose and she tucked it behind her ear. "Of course. And I love you, too."

"I just don't understand how love can curdle so much that someone could kill for it," I said. "I mean, I loved Mary, then our marriage fell apart and I realized I didn't love her anymore. But I never would have hurt her."

"That's you, Steve," she said. Her smile was the kind that reached all the way up to her eyes. "You're controlled by a different kind of passion."

"What do you mean?"

"The term curiosity killed the cat? You're that cat. You have a passion for digging into things, for finding the truth, even if sometimes that leads you down the wrong path."

I took her hand in mine. It was soft, except for a callus where her finger regularly pressed the shutter button on her camera. Her nails were perfectly shaped, polished in silver with white tips. "So you're saying I don't love you enough to want to kill you?"

"I certainly hope you never want to do that," she said. "I'm just saying that different peoples' brains are wired differently."

"And what do you feel passionate about? Photography? Teaching?"

"I went through some heavy-duty therapy after my marriage to Philip ended," she said. "I was worried that something was wrong with me, that I kept making bad choices in romance, that maybe I was too selfish to commit to someone."

"I don't see that," I said. "You're not selfish at all."

She nodded. "My therapist helped me see that my passion is a lot like yours—I want to help people, to do good in the world. My photojournalism was an extension of that, and so is my teaching. I feel like through my pictures I was able to provide evidence of injustice, and help make real changes in people's lives. And teaching does the same thing for me, without all the danger of traveling through war zones."

"Though you're willing to take a motorcycle ride on the wild side now and then?"

"With you driving?" She leaned over and kissed me lightly on the lips. "I think that's just the kind of ride I'd like to take."

\* \* \*

Saturday morning dawned gorgeous and sunny, and not as hot as it had been, so Lili and I decided to take a ride up along the canal and find a good place for a picnic. I wore a pair of board shorts and a microfiber fisherman's shirt, with sneakers and white socks with the Eastern College rising sun logo— one of my recent birthday presents from Lili.

She wore a floaty strapless sundress with a light jacket

over her shoulders to protect them from the sun as we drove. While she finished packing a cooler with lunch, I loaded Rochester into the sidecar, then got on myself. As I was adjusting the chin strap of my helmet, Lili stuck the cooler into a slot behind Rochester, then slid in behind me, with her helmet already in place.

She wrapped her arms around my waist as I turned the bike on. It was the first time I'd ridden with someone else, and I went slowly at first, as I had the first time I rode with Rochester. The aerodynamics of the bike changed with the extra weight, and I had to lean farther into turns than I had before. I tried to ignore the distraction of Lili behind me, her body up against mine, her hands around my waist.

I drove the way I usually went to Eastern, turning right out of River Bend, heading toward the Delaware, and then left on the River Road. By then I felt better, and that old feeling of flying kicked in. I accelerated a bit as we zoomed past new suburban developments in between fields and farmhouses.

I slowed as we approached an abandoned lock that had been turned into a mini-park, turning carefully from the paved road to the gravel parking lot, and then pulling up to a stop at a parking space parallel to the road. We were the only people there and so I let Rochester off his leash so he could race around sniffing madly.

Before I could take off my helmet, Lili insisted on taking a couple of photographs of me on the bike. I posed with my hands gripping the handlebars, trying to look like a real biker rather than the suburban wannabe that Travis at the bike shop had seen in me. When I saw the pictures I realized I wasn't very successful at it, but Lili was happy with the shots so I didn't complain.

While I threw a branch for Rochester to retrieve, Lili spread out an old quilt and laid out sandwiches and fruit, with a couple of biscuits for Rochester. As befits his moniker as the golden thiever, he grabbed the branch and refused to return it to me, holding it in both his paws and gnawing on the end.

He gave up on the branch when we started to eat, positioning himself between Lili and me so that he could accept tidbits from each of us. We were relaxing in the sun when my phone rang from a local number I didn't recognize. Out of habit, I answered.

"Steve? It's Peggy Landsea."

I looked over at Lili, who was watching me. "Hey, Peggy. How are you holding up?"

"About as well as can be expected. I've been cooped up in the house for so long I feel like I haven't breathed fresh air in days. I could use some company. You feel like coming over?"

"How about late this afternoon?" I asked. "My girlfriend and I are upriver a few miles having a picnic."

"Oh, I don't want to disturb you," she said. "We can do it another day."

I looked over at Lili. "If you go over to Levittown you could bring us back Italian from that place I like on Route 13," she said.

"No, this afternoon is good," I said to Peggy. "Say four o'clock?"

We agreed, and I hung up. "She's got you roped in, hasn't she?" Lili asked. "I can see it in your face."

I started to protest, but she stopped me.

"That's okay. I'm not jealous or anything. I know you're a knight errant in search of damsels to protect and truths to uncover, and I love you for it." She smiled. "I wish there was something else we could call each other, though. Boyfriend and girlfriend sound so juvenile. And if you suggest boo or bae I might have to hit you."

"I agree with you. Partner's too businesslike, and significant other sounds like something for a tax return." I cocked my head. "You want to be my lady?"

"And you can be my man," she said.

We both began to laugh. "It makes us sound like we've

just stepped out of some 1970s song," I said. "You could call me your beau. I like that."

"Short for bozo?" Her eyes danced. "How about we settle on something like 'my love'? That works for both of us."

"I can do that, my love," I said. The words rolled off my tongue easily.

Then Rochester came to nose his way between us. "You're my love, too," I said, scratching behind his ears. "No need to be jealous."

# 12 – Liberty

We relaxed at the picnic area for a while longer, the three of us stretched out on an oversized blanket, until the sun got too hot. "How do you like being a biker babe?" I asked Lili, as we packed up for the ride home.

"It's good except for the helmet hair," she said. "I'm going to need to condition the hell out of my curls to get them back in shape."

"You're always lovely to me," I said. "Even with your hair plastered down on your head."

"I wish I could say the same to you," she said, and laughed.

Back home, Lili said she was going to take a nap, and before I left for Peggy's she told me what she wanted from the Italian restaurant, Geppetto's. It was an old school place I'd gone to with my parents, and I'd introduced Lili to it the year before.

I was happy to take the BMW to Peggy's and ride in air conditioned comfort, and Rochester seemed content to curl up on the passenger seat without any restraints.

When Peggy came to the door, she looked better than she had the last time I'd seen her — not so tired, and when she smiled I could see a hint of the old Peggy. She'd pulled her brown hair up into a ponytail, and with no makeup, she looked at least ten years younger.

"I spoke to Hunter yesterday," she said, as she led Rochester and me into the living room. "He says you might be able to find someone else who had a motive to kill Carl? Did you find something in those emails?"

"I'm still working on it," I said. "But that guy you mentioned, Frank Diehl, he sounds like he had a motive to kill Carl. Diehl was in prison until a couple of months before Carl died. Do you know if Carl saw him?"

"Frank didn't come to the house," Peggy said. "But Carl was out on the bike every weekend, and he'd never tell me who he talked to or hung out with. It used to be that I'd go with him, and I got to know some of the other guys and their wives or girlfriends. I felt left out when he wouldn't take me with him."

Once again, I worried that Peggy had been the one to kill Carl—to be on her own, instead of under the thumb of a manipulator.

As if she was reading my mind, she said, "I didn't kill him, you know." She shifted on the sofa, pulling her knees up to her chest. "Hunter has never asked me that question outright, because I guess he's afraid of what I might say. Carl may have been a jerk, but he got me out of Club Hott, and I was grateful for that. I was going to go back to work, you know, right before he died. Probably couldn't get a legal secretary job, but I didn't care, I'd work at anything just to get my old self back."

My heart jumped a bit then. I remembered Peggy's old self, and I wanted to help her return to it. "I'll let you know as soon as I have something concrete about Frank Diehl," I said.

"Thanks, Steve. It feels good to have someone who remembers me and believes in me."

Rochester came over to join us, his big tail waving like mad, and on his way he knocked over a big pile of mail on the coffee table. "Sorry about that," I said, as I leaned over to pick it all up.

"It's my fault. I haven't been willing to look at the mail for a long time. Probably a ton of bills I'm back due on." She shrugged. "Won't matter if they put me in jail."

"You can't let yourself think like that, Peggy," I said. "Come on, I'll help you. At least we can separate out the junk and figure out what you need to pay attention to."

We sat side by side on the floor in front of the coffee table, and it was almost like we were teenagers again. I began making a pile of junk mail, and handing Peggy the bills.

"Carl was going to college?" I asked. I held up a piece of mail from Liberty Bell University.

Peggy snorted. "Not on your life."

"Mind if I open it?"

"Go ahead. I'm going to get my checkbook and pay some of these bills while you're here to keep me accountable."

I slit open the envelope and pulled out a single piece of paper. It was a transcript from LBU, showing that Carl had registered for a freshman composition class in the spring term, which he had failed.

When I looked more closely I realized there was a typo on the page. It was addressed to Carol Landsea, not Carl. "Look at this," I said, showing the page to Peggy when she returned with her checkbook. "Carl wasn't a cross-dresser, was he?"

"Not in this lifetime." She looked at the sheet. "And this isn't his social security number, either. I know, I've had to fill it out enough times lately."

I wondered if the number there was one of the ones from the spreadsheet that LoveMySled28 had sent Carl. "Can I take this home with me?" I asked.

She shrugged. "Sure, if you want to."

I spent the next half hour sorting through mail while Peggy wrote checks. Carl had left enough in their joint checking account to cover her for a few months, but she'd eventually need to get a job—that is, if she wasn't in prison.

By the time we were done, she had paid the cable, the phone, the electric, and a bunch of credit card bills under her name and Carl's.

Before I left, I called Geppetto's and placed a to-go order. "Thanks for coming over, Steve," Peggy said. "I appreciate it. I didn't realize how far behind I had gotten on the mail and the bills."

"Glad to be of help. And I'll let you know when I find out anything else useful."

She kissed my cheek and petted Rochester, and the dog and I drove down to Geppetto's, the kind of place with leatherette booths, posters of Italy on the walls, and placemats with maps of the country on the tables.

My mother had a specific dish she ordered at each kind of restaurant. Chinese, she got shrimp with lobster sauce. Seafood, she'd get shrimp scampi. And at an Italian place, it was chicken parmigiana. I'd ordered that dish in her memory, with the tortellini alla panna for Lili, a half dozen garlic rolls, and a pair of cannoli.

I had to put the bag of food in the back hatch because the smell was too tantalizing and Rochester would have gone nuts. As it was, he kept trying to scramble into the back to get to the food, and a couple of times I had to tug on his collar and get him back into his seat.

Back home, I spread the feast out on the kitchen table. "You used to go to this place as a kid?" Lili asked.

"Yup. My dad commuted to work with a couple of guys from Levittown, and they were always recommending restaurants to him. Local joints, of course – back then we didn't have all these national chain places like we have today. If you went to an Italian restaurant, it was owned by an Italian family and everybody who worked there was related. We used to go to a Greek diner sometimes, and a Chinese place, but that was about it for ethnic food."

"We moved around so much that we never were able to establish favorite restaurants," Lili said. "And besides, my mom was such a good cook that it was hard to justify going out to eat."

"My mom wasn't a cook," I said. "And she figured Friday was her night off, after working all week. She loved seafood, but my father refused to go to seafood restaurants on Friday nights because of all the mackerel snappers."

"And what, pray tell, are those? A special kind of fish?"

I laughed. "No, it was my father's nickname for Catholics who couldn't eat meat on Fridays., which was still a big thing when I was a kid. He was worried that all the Catholics would fill up the seafood restaurants on Friday nights, so if my mom wanted shrimp or lobster sometime, it had to be on a different night."

I fed Rochester bits of chicken but resisted giving him any of the garlic rolls, because I knew that garlic was toxic to dogs, and even though I probably could have gotten away with giving him a small taste, I didn't want to risk a visit to the vet's emergency room. Been there, done that.

After dinner, Lili went upstairs and I took a quick look at the spreadsheet of Social Security numbers and compared them to the transcript that had come in the mail to Birch Valley. Sure enough, the number Carl had used to register at Liberty Bell U was one of them. Had he registered under the name Carol? Or was that just a typo the college had made?

I called Peggy. "Did you and Carl have a joint checking account?" I asked.

"Yup. I didn't make any money after I stopped dancing, so Carl paid all the bills."

"Can you see if Carl ever got a deposit from Liberty Bell University?"

"Why would they have paid him? He didn't work there."

"There's a scam you can run," I said. "You register for a class at a college like Liberty Bell U. You get financial aid, like a Pell Grant. That money goes to the college, and they take out the cost of the tuition and then send the remainder to the student."

"You think Carl did that?"

"I'm not sure. But if the college gave him some money, then that's a good explanation for it."

"When do you think this would have happened?" she asked. I heard her flipping through pages in the background.

"Probably January," I said.

"Son of a gun," Peggy said a moment later. "Here it is. A little over four thousand dollars, in mid-January." She blew out a breath. "I never thought Carl would be sharp enough to figure something like this out."

"I don't think he was behind it," I said. "I think it's something to do with the Levitt's Angels. Did you know a guy who used the email address of LoveMySled28?"

"I only knew the guys by their names, not their email addresses," she said.

I told Peggy I'd get back to her, and hung up. Who was LoveMySled28? How could I find that out without trying to hack into his email server? I was mulling over that question when Lili came into the bedroom. "Want to watch a movie?" she asked. "There's a bunch of new ones on Netflix."

I'd rather watch a movie with Lili any time rather than risk falling down the slippery slope into hacking, so I postponed looking for LoveMySled and said, "Sure, let's pick one."

We spent the next couple of hours watching a mindless romantic comedy, and the only problem I had with it was how unrealistic it was. If you were lucky, you found someone like Lili to fall in love with and share your life with. If you weren't, you could end up the way Peggy Doyle had, living with jerks and then a widow three times over.

There was probably something to be said for getting free of those bad situations, though I knew that even ending a bad marriage, as I'd had with Mary, came with a lot of pain and sadness. I could only imagine what it must be like to go through that three times. I hoped I never had to experience it again.

# 13 – A Good Hand

I didn't get to look for LoveMySled Saturday night after the movie was over, and Sunday morning I had to get ready for the poker run. I loaded Rochester into the sidecar and we trolled down the street Bob Freehl's house.

The day was warm and partly cloudy, and Bob said it was perfect weather for the poker run. "Not too much sun to cause a glare on the road, or to roast you," he said, as I idled my bike in his driveway while he got ready.

"You're bringing the dog with you? Really?"

"Why not? It took him a while, but he likes the sidecar."

Bob snorted, then swung his leg over his bike and turned it on. He let me take the lead for a while as we drove to Willow Grove Mall, where we'd sign in and get our first card, and when we arrived he said that for a newbie I handled the bike pretty well.

The mall parking lot was filled with bikes and bikers, and I kept Rochester on a tight leash as we walked over to the registration table. I looked around for anyone wearing the Levitt's Angels logo on shirts or jackets but I didn't see any.

Most of those around us looked like weekend warriors —older guys with tricked-out bikes who soothed a bit of midlife crisis with a fancy motorcycle and the illusion that they were wild enough to rebel against suburban conformity.

Guys like Carl, though, were the real rebels, because they didn't have the advantages that the men in Brooks Brothers polo shirts and expensive leathers did. In the end, though, weren't we all the same, looking for a bit of freedom from constricting lives?

I didn't feel trapped the way I knew some of my friends did. A couple of my college friends complained about wives who weren't interested in sex anymore, jobs that felt like tombs, and kids who caused constant worry. For guys like that, a bike could represent real freedom.

I had a job I liked that paid me well, a relationship with Lili that still felt new and exciting, and the love of a good dog. I'd been able to reinvent myself after prison. So what was so appealing to me about the motorcycle? Did I really want to buy one and ride it around, or was I playing a part as I looked for information about Carl Landsea's murder?

If that second idea was the real one, then I was striking out. None of the guys I saw in the mall parking lot looked like a Levitt's Angel, and I worried that I was wasting an entire day looking for evidence that wasn't there for me to find.

I could complain about that, or I could enjoy the ride. I chose the second option. Bob took the lead as we headed up

Route 611 to our first stop, at the Mercer Museum in Doylestown. It was a towering concrete castle where I'd gone on school field trips. It collected the objects that documented the lives and tasks of early Americans prior to the Industrial Revolution. I thought Lili might like to visit, and that she'd find interesting stuff to photograph, and I made a mental note to talk about it with her.

Rochester wasn't the only dog on the run, and he sniffed a female yellow lab while we waited in line in the museum's parking lot. The lab rolled onto her back and Rochester got up close and personal with her, but she didn't seem to mind. "She's a love sponge," the guy with her said.

"Yeah, mine is too," I said. "How's yours with the bike? Mine is just getting accustomed to the sidecar."

"She rides pillion behind me, with her paws up on my shoulders," he said. "I've got a seat back there with a harness, and she loves the sled as much as I do."

The word sled jumped out at me. "Forgive me, 'cause I'm new at this," I said. "But do a lot of guys call their bikes sleds?"

He shrugged. "It's one of those terms," he said. "Ride, beast, old lady. Different guys have different terms."

"You seem to know your stuff," I said. "Would you mind if I emailed you a question once in a while?"

"No problem. I love talking about bikes." He dug a card out of his wallet and handed it to me. "I do home inspections for a living, so let me know if you ever need my services."

I took the card, and noticed that the email address was a business one, brian@homeservices.com. Could he also be LoveMySled28?

"Thanks," I said.

"Keep the rubber side down," he said, and held out his hand for a fist bump.

I returned the gesture, and a few minutes later Bob and I picked up our second cards and then continued up Route 611 to Easton. As Bob had said, it was a good day to be out on a bike—not too hot, and the Sunday traffic was light.

As I rode, I thought about how I could track down LoveMySled28. It was an odd enough phrase that I could do a simple Google search, and then if necessary dive into some of my more esoteric databases. Rochester leaned over and nuzzled me, reminding me that I was there to enjoy the ride, and I took a couple of deep breaths and focused on the scenery, and on making sure I was riding correctly.

Our next stop was the Crayola Experience in Easton, a combination museum and factory that showed off all the various products the company produced, and how they were made. We didn't go inside, though—just stopped quickly on the street out front and picked up our next card.

I hadn't been to Easton for a few years, and it hadn't changed much - pretty much a postcard of decline in the industrial northeast. Closed stores on the main street, little traffic—though maybe that was because it was a Sunday. Once again, there was no one at the stop who looked like a member of a biker gang. I saw a lot of denim vests and Harley-Davidson T-shirts, but none of them displayed the Levitt's Angels logo.

Then we swung over to Route 212 south, heading to our next stop at the Quakertown Farmer's Market. There was more traffic on 212, lots of lights and stop and go, and I had a lot of time at red lights to think about what in the world I was doing at this event. Was I going to become a recreational biker?

No.

We'd been on the road for nearly two hours by then, and my butt hurt and my arms had begun to ache from clutching the handlebars. I'd only done this because I thought I might run into one of the Levitt's Angels, and it didn't seem like that was happening. I felt pretty stupid by the time Bob and I pulled up at the market.

I flexed my arms and back muscles. I'd pay for this ride

later, I was sure. I was tempted to call it quits, leave Bob to finish the run and head for home with Rochester. But I'd come this far, and I had to finish. I had collected a seven and a pair of eights by then, so I had the potential to put together a decent hand, and my competitive instinct kicked in, too.

I walked Rochester over to the grassy verge next to the market so he could sniff and pee, and while I waited for him to finish I spotted a guy of about my age with a shaved head and a Levitt's Angels jacket.

I let Rochester lead me in the guy's direction. He was standing by his bike, texting on his phone, and when he looked up I said, "So, Levitt's Angels. You must have known Carl Landsea."

He glared at me. "What about it?"

"I knew his wife when we were kids. You think she killed him?"

"What are you, some kind of cop?"

I shook my head. "Just a guy. But because I knew her back when I've been following the story."

"Carl was an asshole," the biker said. "He did all kinds of stupid shit and then ratted out Big Diehl to slide. Whoever killed him did the world a favor."

"You know Big Diehl?"

"Of course. Though nowadays he's like a different

dude. All sappy and taking care of his mom. It's like they cut his balls off in the joint."

He swung his leg over the bike and revved the engine, a clear sign that our conversation was over. Rochester backed away from the sound, and I turned and let him lead us to our bike.

I wasn't happy with the result of that conversation. If this biker dude said that Frank Diehl had changed his attitude in prison, that gave him less motivation to kill Carl. Which put me back at ground zero. I wasn't relishing passing that information on to Hunter or Peggy—I'd felt so good about discovering the beef between Carl and Frank, and I could tell both of them were happy, too.

Rochester hopped right into the sidecar and let me hook up his harness without complaint. "Thought you got lost," Bob said.

"Nah, stopped to talk to somebody. Where do we go from here?"

"Synagogue in Elkins Park."

"Oh, yeah. Beth Sholom. It was designed by Frank Lloyd Wright. I went there once for a college course on American Art and Architecture." I remembered the soaring pyramid shape, the way the light filtered in through the glass. Yet another place to take Lili, I thought.

By the time we made it to Beth Sholom I was worn out, but I still experienced a bit of an adrenaline surge when the volunteer behind the desk handed me my last card. Would it be a seven, giving me two pair? That wasn't a great poker hand, but if the gods were with me it might be worth something.

I was disappointed to get a two, which didn't do anything for my hand. And I'd learned very little on the ride, beyond an introduction to motorcycle slang and some insight into Big Diehl. Unfortunately for Peggy, what I'd learned wasn't going to help her case. If Diehl had turned over a new leaf in prison and was dedicated to taking care of his mom, then he wouldn't have taken out any anger on Carl Landsea.

I was tempted to write the whole day off as a waste, except my registration fee had gone to charity.

Then we got back on the road, and with Rochester beside me I once again focused on the sights around me, and the sheer joy of being out in the world without the shield of a car around me.

It was only another twenty minutes back to the starting point at the Willow Grove Mall, where I picked up my final card, a three. A lousy poker hand, but Bob's was no better. "How was your first poker run?" Bob asked.

"Honestly? My butt hurts," I said. "But I can see why

people love riding."

"Yeah, it gets under your skin," he said. "You want to go for a shorter ride sometime, you let me know."

I thanked him, and we saddled up for the ride back to Stewart's Crossing. At least I'd gotten out in the world for a while, with my dog by my side. I'd settle for that any day, even if meant I had to go back to everything I'd found and look for another suspect in Carl Landsea's murder.

# 14 – Financial Aid

By the time I got home I was exhausted, and I was thrilled when Lili volunteered to feed and walk Rochester. I went upstairs and took a nap, and awoke about an hour later to the smell of Lili's picadillo, a wonderful Cuban dish of ground beef and tomatoes, with raisins added for sweetness.

"How was your bike ride?" she asked, when I came downstairs. "You looked pretty wiped out when you got home."

"It was long," I said. "Probably too long for me to do, given how little time I've actually spent on the bike. But I saw a whole bunch of places I want to go back to with you."

I described everywhere we'd been, and she agreed she'd like to go to the Mercer Museum and Beth Sholom temple. She surprised me, though, with an interest in going to Easton as well. "I think it might be interesting if I can do some comparison between the color of the Crayola factory and what sounds like the grimness of the city," she said. "Maybe after we get back from Wildwood Crest we can start scheduling these trips. Are you going to keep the bike?"

"Today wiped me out. It was fun in parts, don't get me wrong, but I'm not sure I belong on a motorcycle."

I was too tired to do any research after dinner, choosing

to sit up with Lili in bed and watch YouTube videos of a couple of the different singing competitions we followed.

At Friar Lake the next day, though, I had some time and I looked for more information on Frank Diehl. I was surprised to find that he had a Facebook page, where he kept family and friends up to date on his mother's condition. He hadn't restricted his information so I was able to see everything.

He presented himself as a devoted son. He wrote about taking his mom to her doctor's appointments, spending time with her going over old photographs, trying to spur her memory whenever he could.

It was sad, but also sweet, and I had to admit the guy there didn't appear to hold grudges against anyone. He even mentioned that he was grateful for what he'd learned in prison, and how it had enabled him to turn his life around.

With Big Diehl off the suspect list, I was left with the question of LoveMySled28. A Google search led me to a Yahoo group for motorcycle enthusiasts, where someone using that email address posted occasionally, usually in response to a question. He seemed pretty knowledgeable about motorcycles, posting about customized bikes called bobbers, how to use the choke for a motorcycle's carburetor, and so on.

But who was he? Clicking the link for his profile only mentioned that he was a motorcycle enthusiast who rode a Suzuki GSX-R sport bike. I did a quick search on that and was amused to find it referred to as "A favorite of the too-much-testosterone set."

He was articulate, and wrote well, and had a knack for explaining complicated material in a way that even a newbie like me could understand.

Did that mean that he was smart enough to have engineered a financial aid scam like the one Carl had taken part in? I wondered if someone from Carl's email contact list worked at Liberty Bell University, but at least half the entries were first names only, and another quarter were nicknames, like LoveMySled28. I wasted a good hour popping the remaining names into the LBU home page search function, with no result.

I was discouraged when I finished. I had jumped to a conclusion with little evidence behind it, and I needed to go back to the last messages that Carl had deleted and see if I could find anything there.

The only interesting thing I found was a bunch of messages from a woman named Rita about business dealings — invoices and account deposits. I flagged the messages from Rita for further review. What kind of business

170 | Neil S. Plakcy

was he doing with her?

I sat back in my chair, trying to figure out what to do next, and Rochester came over to me with Carl Landsea's address book in his mouth. It was wet with saliva and the dog had chewed a bit of the upper right corner.

I couldn't yell at him, though. It was leather-bound, and something about the hide had probably triggered an atavistic response in him. At least he'd brought it to me before he had destroyed it. I thanked him, ruffled his air, and then wiped the saliva on my pants.

Then I flipped through to the R's, hoping to find Rita there.

No luck. But then again, I didn't know her last name, so I went back to the A's and started there. I had only to get to the C's, though, to find Rita Corcoran, and a cell phone number. The area code was 267, an overlay code for Philadelphia and most of Bucks County. Probably a cell phone, but that didn't matter because I had an account with one of those number trackers that could find out who it belonged to.

Sure enough, Rita D. Corcoran came up, with an address in Newtown, a suburb a few miles inland from Stewart's Crossing. I plugged that into Google Maps and found a street view of a neighborhood of large chateau-style homes, with stone fronts, peaked roofs and multi-car garages. Rita was sure doing well for herself if that was where she lived.

I jumped into the property appraiser's database and discovered that sure enough, Rita D. Corcoran owned the home at that address, which she had purchased two years before for $600,000. I logged into a database I subscribed to which provided financial details for individuals – without their consent, of course.

Rita had put down $120,000 on the property, enough that she wouldn't have to pay private mortgage insurance, which was a wise decision on her part. Then she'd begun making regular payments on the mortgage, usually paying nine thousand dollars a month in addition to what was required. Since transactions over ten grand got extra attention, I wasn't surprised she was sticking below the radar level.

I tried to trace back the source of the founds, but all I got was a message that the funds had come from a non-US financial institution that could not be accessed.

Rita got more and more interesting by the minute. What was a wealthy woman like her doing with a low-life like Carl Landsea? And where did she get that extra cash to pay down her mortgage so quickly? At nearly a hundred grand a year, she'd have the house paid off in another couple of years.

I started trolling social media for information on her. She didn't have a listing on LinkedIn, and none of the many Rita Corcorans on Facebook matched her details. A woman of mystery, indeed.

Fortunately Rochester reminded me that he was more important than this woman I'd never even met, and I played with him on the living room floor for a while, then took him out for his bedtime walk.

Tuesday morning I left Rochester with Joey at Friar Lake and drove into Leighville, the riverfront town where Eastern's main campus was located. I had been an undergraduate there, and the sight of those old stone buildings in the Collegiate Gothic style, all arches and turrets, incited a powerful feeling of nostalgia.

Too bad Peggy Doyle hadn't had the opportunity I had, to attend a very good small college like Eastern, where I reveled in four years of devotion to academic life and began to grow into the person I was meant to be.

Eastern was always hiring—everything from maintenance personnel up to the highest levels of administration, and for faculty and senior administrative jobs a search committee had to be convened, to review applications, conduct phone and in-person interviews, and make final recommendations to the hiring manager.

Because I was both an alumnus and an administrator, I was in much demand for such committees. Faculty hated to serve on them because of the time commitment, but I had to work nine-to-five anyway and I was happy to give back to the institution that had given so much to me. Not only had I gotten a great education, Eastern had welcomed me back after my prison term and my mentors there had opened doors that had led ultimately to my job at Friar Lake.

This committee was convened to search for a new director of student life. That person was responsible for all the social aspects of a student's time at Eastern, everything from providing the popcorn machine for movie nights to supervising student clubs.

I didn't know any of the other members, so we went around the table in a conference room in the science building and introduced ourselves. Two junior faculty members, one in English and one in chemistry, who were probably untenured and so needed to demonstrate their commitment to Eastern by serving on endless committees, along with the pressure to research and publish in their disciplines.

I didn't want to be in their shoes. I was lucky to be able to teach the occasional course as an adjunct, enjoying the teaching and the contact with students without worrying about all those external pressures.

The other three members of the committee were administrators – the chair of the communications department, the assistant director of financial aid, and me. The guy from financial aid, a thirty-something with a neatly trimmed goatee, had agreed to serve as the committee chair. His name was Dave Moretti, and he'd said that he'd been through five searches in the past year. We spent the next hour hashing through the criteria for the position, and then the fire alarm went off in the building and we had to evacuate.

I walked out beside Dave, and while we stood in the shade of a giant maple, waiting for the all clear, I asked, "I took the online training on financial aid and I was surprised to learn about those Pell chaser scams. Is that a big problem for Eastern?"

"Only for our part-time student population," he said. "You know we've started offering a lot more fully online courses, right?"

I nodded. "I'm an adjunct in the English department. I was thinking about taking the training to offer one of those."

"We get a very different population for those courses," he said. "They're open to anyone with a high school diploma and a high enough SAT score. Most of them are taught by adjuncts, so our cost to offer them is pretty low, and students pay by the credit instead of one blanket tuition charge."

"And they're eligible for financial aid?" I asked.

"Not directly from Eastern, but they can apply for Pell grants and other forms of federal aid. That's where the fraud comes in."

"If their grant is higher than the cost of the tuition, Eastern sends them the difference in cash, right?"

"Exactly. And since those online courses are relatively inexpensive—maybe a thousand dollars a course – somebody with a five thousand dollar Pell grant could get a lot of money back."

"According to the video, students were signing up for courses and not doing any work, and walking off with the cash."

"That's why we had to crack down on F grades," Dave said. "We had an audit last year, and had to pay the government back nearly a million dollars in tuition we collected from ghost students. Now, if you get an F because you never signed into the system and didn't do any work, we report you to the government right away. We have to return the tuition revenue, and then the Feds go after the students for the remainder of the grant we dispensed."

A loudspeaker sounded the all clear, and we went back into the conference room and finished our work, and then I returned to Friar Lake. Rochester pretended to be sad that I had abandoned him, though I knew he'd probably had a great time walking around the property with Joey.

"You can't fool me, dog," I said. He went down on his front paws and looked beseechingly at me, and I laughed. Then he rolled over and I scratched his belly, and all was right in his world. It was up to me to do the same for Peggy Doyle.

# 15 – Push

Lili went into Philadelphia that evening for a talk by a photographer at the Philadelphia Photo Arts Center. I sat at the dining room table, opened up my hacker laptop and went looking for information on LoveMySled28 and Rita Corcoran.

I hadn't bothered to put away the laptop, or hide it from Lili, because I was confident that I wasn't doing anything wrong. That evening, though, my fingers tingled and I wondered how far I could go to search for information on Rita and LoveMySled.

I didn't know enough about either of them to attempt a hack on some protected website. Sure, it would be interesting to see if either of them had received money from Liberty Bell University, but it would be illegal to hack into the private college's financial aid department.

Not going there. But what else could I do?

Duh. One of my programs was a reverse email lookup. All you had to do was enter the address and click a button. I put in LoveMySled28 and his address, and waited. I had bought the premium service – well, I hadn't actually bought it, but found a code online that tricked the site into believing I had.

I saw the first and last initials of the person's name, a

teaser really, along with a location—Levittown, Pennsylvania.

I still had to jump through a bunch of hoops, as it checked social media sites, looked for photos online, and so on. Finally I got the full report, though it wasn't much. A couple of phone numbers associated with the account, a photograph of a motorcycle that served as his avatar somewhere, and a name.

Wyatt Lisowski.

I went back to all my emails and searched for that name. One of the things I've noticed about group emails is that some people will enter your name into their address book, and so whatever they enter there shows up in the TO field. For example, one of Lili's friends had added me to her address book as Lili_Eastern_Boyfriend, so that's the way my name showed up in mass emails. Others left the name field blank in the contact information so all that showed was my email address.

That was the case with Wyatt Lisowski. On some lists, he was there by name, and on others by email, but both monikers resolved to the same email address.

Then I began trolling social media. Eventually I found a photo of him. He had slicked-back black hair, unruly eyebrows and a weak chin. He had attended Bucks County Community College and Liberty Bell University. He liked vintage punk rock like the Clash, superhero movies and Chinese food.

The Liberty Bell University connection jumped out at me. Had he pulled the same scam that Carl had? Or perhaps he had been a student at the private college, and figured out the financial aid scam, then shared the information with his biker buddies. He had supplied them with the list of social security numbers – where had he gotten them?

It took more searching, looking into dozens of websites and databases, before I discovered that he had gotten a certificate in medical coding and billing from the community college, which we had always called BC3. He worked for a large medical group in Levittown with a range of different doctors on staff.

I sat back in my chair and considered. If he worked in medical billing, then he had access to all kinds of information about patients. Medicare used a patient's social security number as an identifier, so Wyatt could easily have skimmed those numbers from patient records.

A government investigator could probably determine if all the social security numbers Wyatt had shared were patients of the medical practice where he worked. I might have been able to do the same, but I wasn't going to break in anywhere to do it.

Maybe I was learning something after all I'd been through. I certainly hoped so.

For now, though, I had a working hypothesis. Wyatt had taken at least one course, if not more, at Liberty Bell University, and somehow he had figured out that he could get money back on a Pell grant. Most likely legally – he was a registered student.

Then he had harvested those numbers and set up a scheme, recruiting other Angels to get extra cash. Did he get a cut for sharing that information? Or was he doing it as part of the brotherhood of the bike?

There was no way to know that without breaking into his bank records, which I wasn't going to do. Unless their systems were heavily protected and very up to date, I could hack Liberty Bell U's student records system and cross-reference the list of Levitt's Angels with their records.

The temptation was so strong and it was hard to resist. Fortunately Rochester must have sensed my dilemma, because he came nosing over to me, pressing his head against my thigh and staring up at me with his big brown eyes.

I shut down the laptop and got on the floor to play with him. We tugged on a rope for a while, and then I tossed a plastic yellow ball for him to retrieve. He did that a couple of times, then settled down with the ball in his mouth, unwilling to return it to me.

That's when Lili came home. "Some reason why you're sitting on the floor?" she asked, as she walked in. Rochester immediately gave up on his ball to jump up and greet her.

"I was playing with the dog until he lost interest in me." I stood up. "How was the talk?"

"He wasn't a great speaker but he showed some amazing images," she said. "Have you heard of Eastern State Penitentiary?"

"I've heard some of my students refer to at Eastern College as a prison, but otherwise, no."

"At one time it was the most famous and expensive prison in the world, but now it's a historic site," she said. "He took some awesome photographs of the place, really gave you the sense of what it must have been like to be incarcerated there."

"Forgive me if I'm not that eager to see photos of prisons," I said.

"I had no idea that's what he was going to talk about. And I fully understand your lack of interest. But for me, the technical aspects were fascinating and there are things he's doing that students could incorporate into their own work."

That was one of the many things I loved about Lili, the way she could get so excited by work in her field, and then be able to learn from it, and translate that learning into something she could use in the classroom.

Wednesday morning I considered driving the motorcycle up to Friar Lake. But my heart wasn't in it. I'd enjoyed that feeling of freedom, but it wasn't practical to keep the bike around for the occasional jaunt, and the poker run on Sunday had showed me that long trips were too taxing on my forty-something body.

I was disappointed, too, that I hadn't gotten more insight into bikers in general and the Levitt's Angels in particular. It was time to give it up. I called Rick to see if he could meet me that evening at Pennsy Choppers, but my call went to voice mail.

When I got to Friar Lake, my email inbox was filled with resumes and cover letters of applicants for the job of student affairs director. With Rochester sprawled on the floor beside me I began the tedious process of going through each one and making check marks on the grid the committee had come up with.

One of the criteria was a familiarity with the kind of students who attended Eastern. Most of the kids I went to school with, as well as those I taught, were high achievers in high school—valedictorians or the captain of the debate team or editor of the newspaper.

Most of today's students were unaware of the world at large, cocooned behind our ivied walls, in a way I didn't think I'd been. They were eager to take advantage of social opportunities and turned out in droves for hip-hop concerts and food truck festivals. But they were less interested in attending speeches by guest lecturers who had been the presidents of war-torn countries or authors of books short-listed for the Man Booker Prize.

I kept coming back to Peggy Doyle Landsea as I thought about Eastern and its culture of high achievement. What would have become of Peggy if she'd had the opportunities I had? I was sure there were Eastern alumni in twelve-step programs or scraping by in minimum wage jobs, but they weren't the ones who wrote in to the notes section of the alumni magazine.

I was out walking Rochester at lunch when Rick texted that he could meet me at Pennsy Choppers that evening at six. I texted him a thanks, and left work at four-thirty so I could drop Rochester at home and then ride the bike over to Levittown. I got there around five-fifteen, and Travis wasn't surprised that I had brought the bike back.

"At least you're sharp enough not to buy the bike and then quit," Travis said. "We get a lot of guys who are all gung ho and then a month later they're back, whining about how they love the bike but their wife hates it or they have to work too hard and can't get any time to ride."

"Not necessarily sharp," I said. "But I'm never going to be one of those guys who makes fancy moves on the highway."

"We call them squids," Travis said. "Then there are the posers, the guys who have to have the latest and shiniest gear, but never actually put any miles on the bike."

"You have a nickname for guys like Carl Landsea?"

He nodded. "The DIY nutcase. Don't get me wrong, I work on my own bike, too. But Carl took it to the extreme. He rebuilt his own engine, and he carried this amazing toolkit so he could be ready for anything -- tire blowouts, a gas tank leak, on-the-fly chain tension adjustments." He shook his head. "Only thing he wasn't ready for was the issue with his brakes."

He handed me the paperwork that showed I'd returned the bike, and I walked outside to Rick's truck.

"I was at the county courthouse for a trial this morning, and while I was there I ran into a guy I know from the Falls Township police," he said. "I asked him what he thought about the Black Widow case."

He took a breath. "Here's the thing. They found Margaret Landsea's prints on her husband's bike."

"That's not very strong evidence," I said. "She was his wife. I took Lili out for a ride on the bike on Saturday, so I'm sure her prints are on it. No reason why Peggy couldn't have gone out for a ride with Carl sometime. Where on the bike were the prints?"

"Don't know," Rick said. "But the cops over there in Falls aren't stupid."

"Wasn't the bike messed up in the accident?" I asked.

"You're determined to prove this woman innocent, aren't you?" Rick asked.

"It's more than that. I feel like Rochester when he gets his teeth into a bone. He doesn't like to let go. I want to know who killed Carl Landsea. I'd hate to find out it was Peggy, but I need to find the answer."

"You know real police work isn't like that," Rick said. "Sometimes you never know the reason behind a crime, or find the person who did it. Sometimes you know who's guilty but you can't prove it."

"That's the beauty of not being a cop," I said. "I can push as long as I want."

# 16 – Tether to Reality

Rick dropped me at home, and while Lili was upstairs, I opened my hacker laptop and wiggled my fingers. There had to be a way I could make a connection between the social security numbers Wyatt Lisowski had sent Carl, the medical practice where Wyatt worked, and Liberty Bell University.

I scanned through every hacker tool I had. Certain ones, like port scanners, which  detected vulnerabilities in firewalls, were only useful if I was going to mount an attack, which I most definitely was not going to do. The same was true for Linux rootkits, scanning programs that looked for vulnerabilities in web applications, and intruders, which allowed automated attacks on web applications.

All of those were illegal, and dangerous in the possession of someone who had little self-control. Others were less malicious, like spiders, which automatically crawled and mapped websites; repeaters, which allowed you to test an application yourself; and decoders, which either returned encoded data to its original form, or converted data into coded formats.

None of them, though, suited my purpose, and I was frustrated. Rochester sensed me and tried to get me to pay attention to him, but I pushed him away. "Go see Mama Lili," I said. "I'm working here."

He looked at me with mournful eyes. Mama. I remembered MamaHack, one of my friends from the online hacker support group, and how she'd responded to my query about the tingling I felt even when I was looking into legitimate sites. Maybe there'd be something in the group about legitimate ways to find information that might spur something for me.

There wasn't much in the archive, and the group hadn't been very active. I guessed some of the members had either gotten over their problems, as I had for the most part, or gotten into more trouble than an online group could handle.

There was one message from a new member, hookmeup18, who had been suspended from his private high school because he had hacked into the school's database. "I'm sure they're going to expel me," he wrote. "And I know I'm being a moron because I need to fucking graduate, and this is the third private school I've been to in three years."

He didn't have a question, just needed to rant, but I felt obliged to answer him anyway. "Have you considered white hat hacking?" I wrote. "You sound like a smart guy. Study on your own and get your GED and while you're doing that, sign up for one of the non-degree courses in cyber forensics. See if you can channel your talents into something legit."

I searched for a couple of programs he could consider, and pasted the links into my message. When I finished, I sat back and thought about what I'd seen. Did I want to sign up for any of those courses myself? Suppose I couldn't make a success of Friar Lake, and the college president chose to replace me with someone else. What could I do, with my erratic background: technical writing, a bit of college teaching, some fund-raising, and now running a conference center.

And a criminal record, of course. That was going to dog me for the rest of my life.

I envisioned a future with Lili, and I knew that she was growing increasingly worried about her mother, who lived in Miami and was in failing health. We'd talked idly about the possibility of moving down there, if Lili could get a teaching job in the area. I'd never been very enthusiastic, even though I would be happy to leave Pennsylvania winters behind, because I knew I wouldn't be able to duplicate the job I had at Friar Lake anywhere else.

But IT security? Cyber forensics? That was the kind of thing I could do on my own, and my criminal record for hacking might even be a plus. While I had the time and flexibility, should

I sign up for a course or two?

Or would I simply turn what I was learning into a negative, discovering even more ways to snoop around online?

I went back to one of the sites I'd recommended to the kid, and saw a course on how to collect and aggregate data from social media sites. Maybe that would help me learn more about both Wyatt Lisowski and Rita Corcoran.

That sent me into the dark web, where I hunted for a good tool that would collect data from Facebook, Twitter, Instagram and other social media sites, dump it into a file, and then organize it by relevance to my search terms. I downloaded a couple of them and fiddled with each for a while, finally deciding on one that claimed to scrape data in direct defiance of the terms of service of the different sites.

It wasn't quite hacking, but it wasn't a hundred percent legal, either. If I found anything that Hunter ought to see, I'd have to massage the way I acquired it. After all, viewing the information directly through Facebook, for example, wasn't illegal. It was my shortcut that was questionable.

I set it up to run and went upstairs to hang out with Lili for a while. I recalled my earlier thoughts, and asked, "How's your mother doing?"

"Same old complaints. It hurts when she stands up. It hurts when she sits down. The lady in the condo below her plays her music too loud. There's a lot of seaweed on the beach and the management office won't do anything about it because they say it's the city's problem."

She looked at me. "What brought that up?"

"Just thinking about the future." I told her about the online courses in cyber forensics I'd recommended to the kid. "If I got myself certified in something like that I'd be a lot more portable. We could move to Florida if you wanted, if you could get a job there that you'd like. And then you'd be close to your mother."

"That's awfully sweet of you," she said. "For right now, she's doing okay, and Fedi and Sara are close enough in case of emergency." Lili's younger brother and his wife and kids lived a few miles inland from Senora Weinstock's oceanfront condo. "But it's always good to have flexibility."

We snuggled together until Rochester came nosing at us, ready for his bedtime walk. I forgot all about the program I'd set up on the hacking laptop to look for information on Wyatt Lisowski, and only noticed the computer was still on when I went to feed Rochester his breakfast the next morning.

The program had saved a huge text file of data, and I copied it to my flash drive. Then I reset the parameters to "Rita Corcoran," and let it loose. I took the drive with me to Friar Lake, and after spending another morning reviewing cover letters and resumes for the search committee, I was able to take a look at it after lunch.

The data was organized by relevance, starting with references that included both "Wyatt" and "Lisowski." There weren't that many of them, and at least half of them came from Facebook posts where Wyatt had been added to a list, usually of those attending a biker event.

Wyatt was either shy or reluctant to have his picture taken, because he only appeared in one of those posts, a group shot of eight Levitt's Angels with their arms around each other's shoulders. Wyatt was at one end, with Carl Landsea next to him. Big Diehl was at the far end.

The other guys in the photo matched several of the names I had gleaned from reviewing Carl's emails. Then I opened up a spreadsheet and started making notes. When were Wyatt and Carl together? Which posts connected to Wyatt's job, which to the Angels, and which to Liberty Bell University?

I was so caught up in that work that I was surprised when

Joey stuck his head in my office door and said, "I'm closing up soon. You sticking around?"

I looked at the clock and realized it was nearly five. "No, I'll shut down on my end."

That was the kind of thing that often happened when I delved into analyzing data. An old boss of mine had called it getting into the zone, and he'd even forbidden the receptionist from using the public address system to page any of us, because he was afraid that would disrupt our work.

It was scary to recognize I could get so involved in something that I shut the rest of the world out, but I knew I always had Rochester as my tether to reality.

# 17 – Passion and Change

That evening Lili and I sat together over a dinner of fettucine alfredo with grilled chicken strips (a couple of which went to Rochester), garlic bread and a nice Pinot Grigio.

"I'm looking forward to taking a lot of pictures at the beach," she said.

She was wearing another of her strapless sundresses, this one in bright yellow with white polka dots and a swirly skirt. She had teased her hair up into a big bun but a few curls had escaped.

"We say 'down the shore,' you know," I said. "That's the real Jersey way."

"I keep forgetting you were actually born in New Jersey," she said. "Did you go 'down the shore' a lot when you were a kid?"

I nodded. "Almost every summer. We stayed in motels by the beach and I was always either in the pool or the ocean. It's weird—I would make these great friends of kids who were at the same motel, and it was like having the brothers and sisters I didn't have, and then the week would be over and I'd never see them again. Today, kids probably immediately friend each other and Instagram everything they do."

"I might do that myself. It will be great to take pictures for fun. This new Panasonic camera is pretty good, with lots of features I'm still exploring. I've been looking at images online and there's a boardwalk with all kinds of funky signs, and colorful beach umbrellas and wacky 1950s architecture."

"You really do love taking pictures, don't you?"

She looked at me like I had two heads. "Well, duh."

"I mean, I know photojournalism was your career for years, but now you're a professor and a department chair. I forget sometimes how much photography means to you."

"I can't imagine what I'd be doing if I hadn't discovered the power of images," she said. She tucked one of those stray curls back into her bun, and I imagined what fun I could have taking that complicated hairdo down in bed, seeing the curls come wantonly loose.

"Taking pictures carried me through the bad times," she continued. "When I was unhappy in my marriages or after my divorces, when I didn't know what else I could do. I feel terrible for your friend Peggy because I know what she's gone through, and how hard it is to keep starting your life over again."

"Maybe that's why she fell into drugs again," I said.

"Because she didn't have anything left that she felt passionate enough about to use as a life raft."

Lili cocked her head. "Do you feel that way about hacking?"

My immediate reaction was to say no, not at all, but I stopped for a moment and thought. "I'm not sure," I said eventually. "Like photography for you, hacking carried me through some tough times, after Mary's miscarriages. But I always knew that it was a bad thing, that it could get me in trouble, so I had to rein in my enthusiasm for it."

"Then what makes you feel passionate?"

"Well, you, of course," I said, smiling. "And Rochester. I like teaching the occasional course, and I'm intrigued by everything I still have to learn to make Friar Lake a success. But I guess it comes down to the thrill of figuring out puzzles and mysteries."

I told her how I'd lost track of time that afternoon while I was analyzing the data I'd collected about Wyatt Lisowski. "I want to help Peggy, and even though I never knew Carl Landsea and I don't think he was a particularly nice guy, I want to see justice for him." I paused. "But most of all I want to know how all the pieces fit together."

"My puzzle guru in shining armor," Lili said, smiling. She took my hand and squeezed.

She cleaned up the dishes while I went into the dining room and collected the results on Rita Corcoran from the social media analyzer. Then I opened a new window and started putting in the names of the other Angels, adding in additional parameters that would search for connections between them.

As Lili passed me on her way upstairs, she stopped. "You're not taking that laptop with us down the shore, are you?"

I looked up at her. "I wasn't planning to."

"Good. Because I want you to have a vacation, too, and I want us to be present for each other. Try and shut off the phones and the social media and enjoy ourselves."

"I have to do something when you go off to take pictures," I protested. "But you're right, this little baby is too much of a distraction. I promise to leave it behind."

She went upstairs, and I worried that I wouldn't be finished with all my analysis by the time we left for the shore. Could I really stop, knowing that Peggy Doyle's future could be in the balance? If I had to choose between solving a puzzle and being present for Lili which way would I go? I was afraid of what my answer would be.

Friday morning when I checked the HR system, there were no new applicants to review, so I spent most of the day reviewing the data the social media analyzer had come up with. I found that a couple of the other Angels had made posts or tweets that mentioned Liberty Bell University, usually in a snarky way. One had written, "Imagine me going to college at my age. Not."

Did that mean these guys had registered for courses to scam the government out of  financial aid money, the way Carl had? It made sense that if one of them was doing it, the others would have, too.

Late in the afternoon I checked my hacker support group, curious to see if the kid had responded to my message. He had, and he thanked me for the advice. "I talked to my dad about these courses. He's a doctor and he always thought I would go to medical school, too, but my grades suck so bad he's finally accepted I'll barely get into college. He says he's happy I've found a positive way to channel my enthusiasm, LOL. Of course he hopes I'll get a degree and become an honest member of society. I guess some dreams never die, right?"

I wrote back to say that I was glad he and his dad were on the same page, and that I was eager to hear which courses he chose. "I might end up doing the same thing," I wrote. "I've been fighting the urge to hack for ten years by now and it might be time for me to make some changes."

After I sent the message I sat back and considered it. I didn't need to switch careers—things were going well at Friar Lake. But it was always a good idea to have a plan for the future, in case the college had other plans for me, or Lili wanted to move to Florida.

Saturday morning Lili left for a trip to the salon to get prepared for a double date with Rick and his girlfriend Tamsen. Once again I got lost in the data I'd collected, making tiny connections between the Angels, Rita Corcoran and Liberty Bell University. One random comment on Rita's Facebook page led me to discover that she worked at LBU, though I couldn't tell what she did.

That was frustrating. I couldn't find her name anywhere on the LBU website, which meant she probably wasn't a professor there, not even an adjunct. But that left a whole range of staff jobs—she could have been anything from a worker in the college café to the president's personal assistant.

I tried using the basic white pages search I'd done for Carl, where I'd learned about his mother, his sister and his ex-wife. In Rita's case, I discovered that her middle name was Jane and that her ex-husband's name was Gregory Corcoran. She was related to an Anne D. Henderson and a Catherine Doonan. I assumed that if they were her sisters, their maiden name was Doonan, but I couldn't find anything online that proved that.

Her recent addresses weren't very useful. She had lived in Yardley, in Pittsburgh, and then Newtown. She wasn't a biker chick, either. I found no record that she owned a motorcycle, and the only clue I found that connected her with the biker group was when she was in the same place as a couple of the Angels, where one of them had checked in at a bar in New Hope and indicated he was with Rita, among others.

Lili came home from the salon, and I was smart enough to glance up from my research long enough to tell her that she looked terrific—which was true, of course. Then I went back to work, stopping only long enough to feed Rochester and give him his evening meal.

At six-thirty Lili and I left to meet Rick and Tamsen at Le Canal, a French restaurant in New Hope that was only a couple of blocks from the bar where Rita had been with the Angels. On our way to the restaurant, we passed it, and there was a line of motorcycles angled toward the curb as we passed. I had the car windows open, and heard ZZ Top's "Sharp Dressed Man" blasting through the speakers.

Le Canal was a world away from that bar. It was a low-slung building alongside the Delaware Canal, with a wall of picture windows that looked out at the towpath. During the day, the mule barges went right past, tourists peering in the windows at lunch guests, but in the evening the canal was quiet, moonlight sparkling on the water and only the occasional duck paddling past.

We met Rick and Tamsen in the parking lot. Tamsen was a few years younger than Rick and me, a tall, slim woman with shoulder-length blonde hair and a broad smile. She wore an open-necked shirt in light blue oxford cloth with the sleeves rolled up and secured by buttoned tabs, and a pair of white slacks my mother would have called pedal-pushers or capris, and flat sandals with rhinestones on the straps.

She looked as casually elegant as Lili, who'd worn a black dress with a low-cut neck and a swirling skirt, with a diamond pendant around her neck. They hugged and kissed while Rick and I shook hands, both of us looking a lot less formal than the women we were with. Rick wore one of his microfiber shirts and a pair of black jeans, and I was in a polo shirt and khakis. We were the opposite of peacocks, allowing our women to shine.

We were fortunate that our friend Gail Dukowski, who owned the Chocolate Ear pastry shop in the center of Stewart's Crossing, had worked with the chef at Le Canal during their days in New York, so we were always treated well, given a table by the window and comped with an appetizer platter.

"Rick says you guys are going down the shore soon," Tamsen said as we nibbled on grilled mushrooms stuffed manchego cheese and tomato and mushroom flatbreads. "I'm so jealous. I'd love to get away for a while, and Justin loves the ocean."

Lili looked at me, and the same thought passed between us, but Lili voiced it. "Come join us," she said. "I snagged us a two-bedroom cottage on Airbnb, a block from the ocean. Rochester and Rascal would have a blast together. And there's a pull-out couch in the living room for Justin."

Tamsen looked at Rick. "What do you think, coach?"

Rick said, "I'm in this for the long haul. I want to marry you someday, and I want to be Justin's stepdad, though I know I'll never replace Ryan."

Ryan Morgan had died a war hero in Afghanistan when his son was only a few years old, and he'd spent the last years idolizing a photo of his dad in full gear.

"You're sure you wouldn't mind?" Tamsen said. "Us

horning in on your vacation?"

"Steve's already said he's going to be bored while I'm out taking pictures. This way he'll have lots of company."

"We can teach Justin how to boogie board," I said to Rick. "Though I'm not sure I remember all that well myself. It's been a long time."

By the end of our meal, we'd made our plans. As long as Rick could get the week off from the police department, and Tamsen could rearrange a couple of meetings with clients of her advertising specialties business, we'd all have a great week together down the shore.

"You don't think I was too impulsive in inviting them to join us, do you?" Lili asked, as we took a walk along the towpath after dinner. "When I looked at you it seemed like we were thinking the same thing."

Rick and Tamsen had already headed back to Stewart's Crossing, but we'd decided to take a stroll. The humidity had dropped and there was a light breeze coming off the water, and stars spangled the sky above us.

"Not at all. Rick's my best friend, you and Tamsen get along well, and Rochester and Rascal are great pals."

"We'll have a week with Justin, though," she said. "All five of us crammed into that little bungalow with the two dogs."

"Rick and I will take Justin to the beach. You and Tamsen can have some girl time, and I think we'll all get along. If not, then you and I will sneak off for dinner on our own a couple of times."

"Food," Lili groaned. "We're going to have to load up a couple of carts to have enough for everyone. A few dozen eggs, bacon, pancake mix... and that's just for breakfast."

I laughed. "Don't over think it," I said. "You and Tamsen can make up your grocery list together. Remember lots of treats for the dogs."

"It always comes back to Rochester, doesn't it?" Lili said. She laughed and took my hand.

"To the three of us," I said.

# 18 – Social Media

I finally got to talk to Lili about taking a computer forensic course on Sunday morning, over a breakfast of chocolate-chip pancakes. "What do you think?" I asked her. "Should I give it a try? Or would it be too tempting for me?"

"You won't be tempted to hack by taking a course in computer security," she said. "Probably the opposite. I think your instinct is good, that it would satisfy your curiosity without getting you into trouble. And I'm the poster child for career zigzags. I know you've done the same thing, too, so it would be useful for you to have some other credentials under your belt. You never know what the future holds."

"As long as it holds you in it," I said, taking her hand.

"Of course." She smiled at me. "I loved the way Rick was so earnest with Tamsen last night, that he's in it for the long haul and wants to marry her eventually."

"And us? Are we still on the same page about marriage?"

"I'm not closing the door to it," she said. "Right now, if it ain't broke, don't fix it." She looked at me. "And you?"

"I agree. There might be some time in the future when it will be advantageous for us to be married — benefits or Social Security or something like that. But for now, I agree with you, things are good."

She smiled and squeezed my hand. "How's your search for student life director going?"

"Lots of candidates but no one stands out so far." I let go of her hand and fetched Rochester a dental stick from the bag on the counter. I handed it to him and he chewed noisily as I sat back down across from Lili.

"Some of them have written doctoral dissertations on student engagement," I said. "I'm glad I never went on for a PhD. I couldn't imagine getting so involved in something to write a whole manuscript on it."

"I loved doing the research for my dissertation," she said. "Weegee was such a fascinating guy and he conveyed so much in his photographs that I could stare at one for hours and keep coming up with new things to say."

"What was the title of your dissertation again? Something about photo-politics?"

"Weegee and the Photo-politics of Race, Class and Gender," she said. "Very overblown title, of course, but I loved creating that word photo-politics. Someday I hope there'll be an Urban Dictionary entry on that word that references me."

"I can do that for you. The Urban Dictionary's a wiki so I

can create an entry if I want."

"I'd rather it came from someone who stumbled on me," she said. "But it's sweet of you to offer." She stood up and began to clear the table. "What's on your agenda for today?"

"I've been running some software that trolls social media for information on the other Levitt's Angels," I said. "So far it looks like a couple of them have connections to Liberty Bell University, and I think they might all be part of a financial aid scam."

I described the way the scam worked as Lili cleaned up and Rochester nosed the floor for stray tidbits.

After the kitchen was clean and Lili went upstairs, I sat down at my hacker laptop to review the results of the social media search. Rochester sprawled on the floor beside me as I opened a new spreadsheet and began transferring information to it. A half-dozen terms seemed to come up regularly, including "Levitt's Angels," "Levittown," the bike shop Pennsy Choppers, and a couple of organized bike runs like the one I had done with Bob Freehl. I created a column for each one, and every time I found a connection between a person and one of those entities, I made a check mark.

The portrait that began to come together was interesting.

Several of the guys regularly got together for runs, and all of them patronized the bike shop where I'd rented my motorcycle, and where Travis had given me an idea of how Carl's bike could have been messed with.

If all the Angels on my list had the ability to fiddle with Carl's brakes, then all of them had to be suspects in his death. Means, motive and opportunity. Every Angel had the means.

They all had the opportunity, too. They had all been at a party at Pennsy Choppers a couple of days before Carl's fatal accident. The parking lot wrapped around the building, and if Carl had parked in the back, any one of them could have fiddled with his brakes while no one was looking.

Motive was the sticking point. None of the messages or tweets or other information I found pointed to a rivalry between Carl and any of the other Angels. Sure, someone could have gotten jealous and wanted more money from the LBU scam, and if Carl was the conduit to Rita, he might have been able to control who was able to register and how often.

Elise had said that Carl was like her Marine ex-husband, very controlling. One of the other Angels could have rebelled against that attitude. Was someone going to expose the scam, providing a threat to Carl?

Unfortunately, the only person who appeared to have means, motive and opportunity was Peggy Landsea. She was mentioned occasionally in posts as riding pillion with Carl, and she was a smart enough woman to have learned about bike brakes if she wanted to. She had the opportunity, because his bike was at the house when he went to work. Her motive? Perhaps Carl was too controlling, or that anonymous caller to the police was right, and Peggy was being abused.

Getting away from an abusive husband was a huge motivation. Because Peggy wasn't working, she probably had little money of her own. Though I'd seen her pay bills from the checking account she shared with Carl, if she'd chosen to run she couldn't take more than the current balance with her. Through her years of drug abuse and pole dancing, she'd become estranged from her family, and I found no indication anywhere on social media that she had any friends other than people she knew through Carl or the Angels.

If she couldn't run, the only other alternative was to get rid of Carl and inherit his house and whatever he had in the bank. At least, that's the way a prosecutor and a jury would see it.

But she didn't seem to know about the Pell grant scam,

and she said she didn't have access to Carl's email account herself. So if that scheme was connected to Carl's death, that let Peggy off the hook.

A lot of assumptions.

I kept working on my spreadsheet, and I was pleased when Rita Corcoran's name came up in a Facebook post by someone in the admissions department at LBU. A photo had been taken at a holiday party the previous December, and Rita was one of those tagged.

That was verification that I was right, and that Rita worked at LBU. I opened up the post where she was tagged and dropped down the rabbit hole of Facebook research, jumping from page to page and one friend list to another. I finally found a post with a picture of Rita at a restaurant with another woman, the assistant registrar, who had posted, "Lunch with the assistant director of financial aid. Good talk about strengthening the connection between our offices."

Rita wasn't named there, which was why the page hadn't come up in my original search. I pulled up a couple of online pictures where Rita had been identified, and compared them. The hair was the same, a chic shoulder-length bob of brown with blonde highlights, and her nose had a slight twist to it. In all the pictures she dressed similarly, low-necked white blouses under navy blazers. Zooming in, I was even able to identify the same pendant around her neck in a couple of the pictures, a square of some kind of iridescent rock.

Bells started going off in my head. Maybe Rita was the connection between Carl and the Levitt's Angels. Suppose Wyatt Lisowski had gotten hold of those social security numbers through his job in medical billing, and asked his fellow Angels what he could do with them.

Carl knew Wyatt, a student at LBU who was also a member of the Levitt's Angels. How did Wyatt figure out the financial aid scam? I needed to know more about Rita Corcoran to figure out if she was the one who had made the whole scheme come together.

# 19 – Many Motives

Before I could do any more searching on Rita Corcoran, Peggy called. "I've been going through Carl's bank records, like you suggested," she said. "I found three deposits, each about six months apart, from Liberty Bell University."

"And you never knew Carl was taking classes there?"

"I'm sure he didn't. Carl was no kind of student and he used to have to ask me to go over his reports, back when he was a supervisor at the steel mill."

"That's good, Peggy. That adds another piece to the puzzle."

"There's something more, though."

She hesitated, and I didn't want to rush her. Let her say it when she was ready.

"He was sending money to my sister RJ. Lots of money." I heard the plaintiveness in her voice. "Why would he do that?"

"Was she having financial trouble?"

Peggy snorted. "RJ loves to brag about how much money she makes at her job. You met her once, when we were kids. She's the one whose used to tease me about being a college girl." She laughed, though there wasn't any humor in it. "Kind of ironic that she works for a college now."

Something tugged at my brain. "What does the RJ stand for?"

"Rita Jean. She was named after St. Rita of Cascia, patron saint of impossible causes and hopeless circumstances. My mom was pretty desperate by the time RJ was born. She was praying non-stop to Saint Rita to get us out of Trenton. Funny how it took my dad dying for that wish to come true."

Had Peggy been praying to the same saint, to get rid of her husband?

But I couldn't stop to wonder about that because I had one more question to ask. "Is your sister's last name Corcoran?"

"Yeah, she married a loser when she was nineteen and took his name. Eventually she dumped him but she kept the name. How do you know her last name?"

"The name has come up in something I'm working on. I'll tell you more once I figure it all out." The ideas were flying through my brain like the rapid fire of a submachine gun. I tried to slow down and focus. "Would you be willing to give me your sign on and password for your bank account?" I asked.

"I trust you, Steve. Carl's salary stopped when he died, so there isn't that much money in the account, now that I paid all the bills. I'm going to have to get a job soon but I can't do anything with this criminal charge hanging over my head and this shackle around my ankle."

She read out the ID and password, and I wrote them down on a piece of paper by my laptop. I ended the call, promising to get back to her as soon as I had a chance to look through Carl's account.

Rochester began nosing me to go out, and while I didn't want to put down what I was doing, I knew how relentless he could be. I looked at him, and decided he'd be the perfect cover for a visit to Rita Corcoran's house.

One of the great things about having a dog is that he gives you a reason to wander past someone's house, stop and look around while he sniffs and pees. I plugged Rita's address in Newtown into my phone, then hooked up Rochester's leash.

He was surprised that we were getting into the car rather than heading down the street, but he jumped in the front seat and sat on his hind legs as I headed out to the Ferry Road exit from River Bend.

I rolled the window down for him and cranked up the air conditioning to compensate, and he looked out the window as we drove inland for a couple of miles. Then I executed a couple of turns that brought us to Oak Hills, the neighborhood in Newtown where Rita lived. Unlike in

Levittown, there were actually oaks there, and hills. Fortunately the community wasn't gated, so I was able to drive along the winding streets past one huge stone-fronted house after another, each of them embellished with gables and cupolas.

I went slowly past Rita's house. It was two stories, with a central portico, a wing with arched windows to the left and a three-car garage to the right. A couple of young oaks framed the driveway, and flower beds under the windows rioted with pink and white azaleas.

A block away, I found a parking spot at the end of a cul-de-sac, and I pulled up and took Rochester out on his leash. We walked slowly back toward Rita's house, Rochester excited by all the new scents and messages from unfamiliar dogs. I didn't tug him along  like I usually did, because I wanted to establish a pattern of slow movement, in case anyone happened to be watching through one of those multi-paned windows.

Garbage and recycling must be scheduled for Mondays, because Rita and many of her neighbors already had their bins and cans out, and Rochester was eager to sniff each of them. The recycling bins were rectangular, made of dark blue plastic, without lids. You could get a real sense of what the neighbors ate and bought by scanning them.

I saw glass wine bottles from The Velvet Devil merlot and a mix of Sangiovese and Shiraz called The Blood of Hipsters. Piles of *New York Times* and *Wall Street Journals*, along with a stack of the distinctive salmon pink of the *Financial Times*. Lots of bottles of designer water, empty granola bar boxes and almond milk cartons.

When we got to Rita's house, I peered down at the contents of Rita's recycling bin, while Rochester paused to sniff and pee. Right on top was a presentation folder with the Liberty Bell University logo on the font. I took a quick look around and didn't see anyone watching. I reached down and picked up the folder.

It was empty — except for a business card in a slot on the inner right side. *Rita J. Corcoran, Assistant Director of Financial Aid.*

I pulled out the card and dropped the folder back in the recycle bin. That was the confirmation that Rita was the missing link I needed. Rita was Carl's sister-in-law, and she worked at LBU. Wyatt had sent those social security numbers to Carl in that encrypted spreadsheet, and Carl could have asked Rita what to do with them.

Rochester and I circled around the neighborhood, and as he took in all the different scents, I thought about how I could implicate Rita Corcoran in the financial aid scam going on at Liberty Bell University.

I could apply myself, of course. See how easy it was to figure out the FAFSA. But if I was being honest, I probably made too much money to qualify for a Pell Grant, and I wasn't going to go so far as to falsify my information.

Did I know anybody broke enough that I could recruit? But I didn't want to encourage anyone to break the law.

Another thought jumped into my head. Suppose Carl and Wyatt had concocted this scheme themselves, and Rita had figured it out and was going to report back to her superiors at LBU. Maybe Carl threatened her and she had killed him to protect herself.

When I got home, I used the information Peggy had given me to log in to Carl's bank account. He had gotten about $4,000 each time over three semesters, but it looked like he was giving Rita a commission --- about fifty percent of the net amount he received, shortly after each of the three deposits from Liberty Bell University.

Rita had made an easy two grand by rubber-stamping his paperwork. When I added in all the other Angels, and the number of social security numbers Wyatt Lisowski had come up with, Rita was pulling in real money. Two hundred fake IDs times two grand a pop, with the possibility of multiple registrations by the same person.

Was it enough to support her lifestyle, though? She probably didn't make much money working for LBU. Peggy had said that Rita's ex was a loser, so it was unlikely he was paying her much alimony, if any at all.

I exported Carl's bank records to a spreadsheet and started manipulating the columns, looking for other suspicious transactions. He had a PayPal account, and he regularly pulled money down from that account into his bank. I went back online and clicked on a transaction.

It was a vendor payment from Liberty Bell University, for something called IT consulting. That made me laugh. Carl seemed like the kind of guy who could barely manage his own online transactions, not someone you'd hire for IT work.

The amount was $990, which immediately set off a red flag. At Eastern, I had the authority to make purchases and pay invoices up to a thousand-dollar limit. Anything over that required a signature from my supervisor, the vice president for external affairs. If Rita was the one at LBU paying Carl, then it made sense she'd keep the amount under a thousand dollars.

I went back to Carl's bank account, and found a PayPal payment twice a month for the last two years. Each of the PayPal deposits matched the email invoices he had sent to Rita, and then to a payment a day or two later to her—in this case, eighty percent of the invoice amount. In all, Rita had netted about $19,000 tax free from the transactions.

Had Rita done the same thing with other members of the Levitt's Angels? If she had, we were talking about an extra hundred grand a year if she recruited ten guys for the same scam. Enough to provide the funds she'd been using to pay down her mortgage so quickly.

I remembered what Elise Lewis had said, that her ex-boyfriend Phil had told her Carl was cheating on Peggy, with a woman who'd surprise Elise. Elise had thought that meant the woman was either prettier or smarter than she'd expect. But it would be a surprise, too, if Carl was having an affair with his sister-in-law.

Was that possible? Rita was an attractive woman, and she resembled Peggy in superficial ways—the same perky nose and sprinkle of freckles. But she was younger and her face and body looked less lived-in than Peggy's. She dressed well, wore makeup effectively, and had a high gloss. Maybe Carl found that attractive, fooling around with a younger, better-looking version of his wife.

What did Rita get out of it? The chance to screw up her sister's marriage?

I realized that from the beginning of this investigation, I'd had the idea that Carl Landsea was a loser. That's what

Hunter had called him, and it had never occurred to me to look at him objectively.

I pulled up a bunch of pictures of Carl and scanned them. He had a handsome face, and the wrinkles across his forehead and laugh lines around the edges of his mouth gave him character. In most pictures his hair was neatly trimmed, and he was clean shaven. For a guy in his late forties, he looked pretty good. He didn't have much of a beer gut, and in one picture he was wearing a sleeveless T-shirt and his tattooed biceps were ropy.

Maybe he wasn't as much of a loser as Hunter had said. When he began dating Peggy, he had a solid job at the steel mill. Sure, he had a police record, but so did I. I could see how women would find the mix of his good looks, his motorcycle and the tinge of danger very attractive.

But could I prove that Carl and Rita were having an affair?

I looked to Rochester for advice, but he was busy chewing. Then I realized he'd finished with the dental stick and had a piece of paper in his jaws. "Come on, boy, you know you can't chew paper," I said, tugging it away from him. "Too much fiber for you."

It was a credit card receipt for the dinner the night before at Le Canal. "You may be onto something, boy," I said.

A guy I worked with in California had been stepping out on his wife, and she'd hired a private detective to follow him. It was too late for that, but I remembered that when she did sue for divorce, she found a lot of evidence in her husband's credit card receipts. Could I discover the same thing about Carl?

I logged back into his bank account and realized that he had a credit card from the same bank, and I was able to click the link on the left-hand menu to see all his transactions.

There hadn't been any since his death, of course. Peggy must have had her own card. I tracked back through grocery and gas charges, until I found one for the Newtown Arms, a fancy restaurant in a converted colonial-era farmhouse. They specialized in farm-to-table cuisine, growing much of what they served in their own gardens.

I'd wanted to go there with Lili until I saw the prices on the menu, then put it aside for a special occasion. Starters began in the double digits, and a steak was forty-five bucks — with side dishes extra.

From the tab on the receipt, it looked like Carl had been there with a guest, and I strongly doubted he'd taken Peggy there. Paging backwards, I found a couple of purchases of lingerie online, as well as a few receipts from an expensive jewelry store in Newtown.

That solved the question of what Carl had been doing with the extra cash he'd made through the scams with Rita.

I'd have to confirm with Peggy that those dinners and gifts hadn't been presents to her, but I was already pretty sure of the answer. It was nearly ten o'clock by then, too late to call Peggy with difficult news.

If Carl and Rita were having an affair, that may have been how Rita roped Carl into the two scams at Liberty Bell University. I went back to one of the lessons I'd learned from Rick about the motives for murder. He'd conveniently categorized them as the four L's – love, lust, lucre and loathing.

Rita could have killed Carl because he'd fallen out of love with her, or because he refused to leave his wife for her. Maybe he wanted to stop participating in the LBU scams with Rita – he'd had a couple of brushes with the law, particularly the last one with Big Diehl, and that might have made him scared about doing anything that might put him in jail.

If Rita knew he'd flipped on his former friend, she might have killed him, or had him killed, to protect herself. Too many motives, and my head started to spin.

I looked over to Rochester. "What do you think, boy? You have any ideas on what's going on?"

He looked up at me, yawned, and rolled over on his

belly for a rub.

# 20 – Golden Eggs

Monday morning I dropped Rochester at Friar Lake with Joey, and drove into Leighville to meet with the hiring committee in a conference room on the Eastern campus.

We had a series of Skype calls set up with our semi-finalists, and my ears perked up when one of the candidates spoke about working at a for-profit college like Liberty Bell University.

"It's very challenging to create engaging programs for students who never come to campus," she said. "How do you develop a sense of community between people who never meet face to face? I focused on creating interactive online programming like discussion groups for first-time in college students, for veterans, and other special interest groups. Interestingly, I worked closely with our financial aid office, trying to discover which students were actually committed to college, versus those who were taking their Pell grant money without doing any work."

Dave Moretti, the guy from financial aid, nodded along. "That's an interesting approach. We've been having some of the same problems at Eastern with Pell scammers and ghost students, though of course not as much as institutions with a lower tuition cost."

I wondered which of the Angels had been the first to participate in Rita's scam. I guessed it was Carl, because she knew him through Peggy, but I made a note to go back over the social media posts I'd found and see if any of the Angels had posted anything about LBU before Carl had accepted his first payment.

The interviews took up most of the morning, and then we had to discuss each candidate and choose which ones we wanted to bring in for face-to-face meetings. When we got to that point, I had to mention that I'd be out of town the following week on vacation. That reminded me that I had to finish up on what I was doing for Hunter Thirkell and Peggy Landsea before I left, as I'd promised Lili I wouldn't take my hacker laptop, and that I'd do my best to be present during our vacation.

With Lili beside me, accompanied by Rick and Tamsen, Justin, Rochester and Rascal, that would not be a problem.

That evening Lili chatted about the vacation as I prepared dinner. "Tamsen and I are making plans to do things together," she said. "We've made reservations at family-friendly restaurants for the five of us a couple of times, and the rest of the time we'll alternate nights with Justin so each couple gets some time together."

"We need to stock up on treats for Rochester and

Rascal," I said from the stove. Rochester recognized his name, and the word "treat," and immediately came up and nuzzled my leg.

"You said the word," Lili said, laughing. "Now you've got to follow through."

It was time for him to get one of his dental sticks anyway, so I gave it to him and he took it into the living room to chew away. I worked on the spreadsheets for a while that evening, and eventually went upstairs, where Lili and I cuddled for a while, until Rochester demanded his last walk. As we strolled down the dark, humid streets of River Bend, I looked up at lit windows and wondered what was going on behind them. Happy couples? Angry ones? Husbands and wives hiding secrets from each other?

Fortunately Rochester reminded me that our real purpose was so that he could sniff and pee on interesting places, and I gave up wondering about other people's lives and focused on my own.

It was Monday night, and we'd be leaving early Sunday morning for the trip down the shore. Our Airbnb rental began that day, and ran until Saturday evening, when we'd leave to return home.

That meant I had the rest of the week to figure out what had happened to Carl Landsea.

Tuesday morning I called Peggy. "Mind if I stop by on my way to work?" I asked her. Levittown was the other direction from Friar Lake, so it was quite a detour, but I wanted to ask Peggy my questions face to face, rather than over an impersonal phone call.

"Sure. I'm not doing anything."

When I got off Route 13 to head to Birch Valley, I spotted a Dunkin' Donuts, and I went through the drive-through and picked up a half dozen donuts and a pair of coffees. I figured Peggy could use the sugar and caffeine to get through our conversation.

"You didn't have to bring anything," she said, when she took the box of donuts from me. "Though I appreciate it."

Rochester and I followed her into the kitchen, where we sat at the table and dug into the donuts and the coffee. "What brings you over here?" she asked. "Must be something bad that you didn't want to tell me over the phone."

"Kind of," I said. "Have you ever been to the Newtown Arms restaurant in Newtown?"

She shook her head.

"Carl ever give you any fancy lingerie or jewelry?"

"What's this about?" She finally showed some emotion. Maybe it was the sugar acting, or the realization of what had been going on.

"I think in addition to working with your sister on this Liberty Bell scam, he was having an affair with her."

She slammed her cup of coffee down on the table. "That bitch. My own sister. Though I can't say I'm surprised, in the end. She always was a jealous little thing."

"I'm sorry, Peggy," I said.

"Do you think she killed him?" Peggy asked.

"Hard to see a motive right now," I said. I told her I thought Rita was behind the financial aid scheme, and that she had also been collecting fake invoices from him and having the college pay him for non-existent work. "Between those two things, she was making a lot of money from him."

"I wouldn't put anything past her. You know that story about the goose that laid the golden egg, right?"

I nodded.

"The goose gets killed in the end. Just like Carl."

# 21 – Vulnerability

As I drove up to Friar Lake, I went back over my conversation with Peggy. It seemed like Carl's affair was news to her, but how could she have been so oblivious?

I had gone over the receipts from the Newtown Arms with her, but she said Carl often told her he was going out with his biker buddies, and she assumed that's where he was the nights he was out with Rita.

When I got to the office I engaged in a flurry of emails with my fellow committee members about the questions for our face to face meetings with the candidates on Thursday.

That kept me busy throughout the morning, and it wasn't until I was out walking Rochester at lunch that I went back to Peggy's situation. What else could I do to research what Carl was up to?

I wanted to know more about Liberty Bell University, and how it easy it might be to scam them. But how could I learn that? Rochester was tugging at his leash, straining to get over to the base of a tree, and I followed him over there. I spotted a broken piece of a keychain, a couple of metal links, and picked it up before he could swallow it.

Links. LinkedIn. I had set up a profile on the site soon after it opened, though I didn't do much with it. I accepted connection requests from people I knew, other educators, and fellow Eastern alumni, and that was about it.

But as soon as we got back to the office, I tried to log in to the site. Of course I'd forgotten my password, and had to jump through a couple of hoops to reset it, but eventually I got in. I did a search among my contacts to see if any had connections to Liberty Bell University, and found a name that seemed familiar.

Dorothy "Dee" Gamay had been an adjunct instructor in the English department when I first began teaching there myself, and I often saw her in the department lounge between classes. She had a habit of answering her phone with her name, and I remembered once she'd been insulted that someone began speaking to her immediately in Spanish.

I had refrained at the time from telling her that "digame," pronounced like her name, meant "talk to me" in Spanish, so it wasn't surprising that someone followed her instructions.

Her profile indicated that she taught English composition for Liberty Bell University, among other institutions. She had stopped teaching at Eastern a couple of years before, though, so I clicked the button that allowed me to send her a message through LI.

"Hi, Dee, Steve Levitan here. We used to teach together

in Eastern's English department, and I'm looking to pick up some adjunct work. I see that you've been teaching at Liberty Bell U. What's it like? I'd appreciate any advice."

I sent the message through and went back to my college email folder, where I was reminded that I still had a couple of those course modules to complete, and I worked through another three before it was time to head for home.

That evening, while Lili was out shopping for bathing suits with Tamsen, I scanned back through all the results from social media accounts of Carl and the other Angels to see who was the first to mention Liberty Bell University. Though the first was an Angel named Ed Antes, it came a full semester after the first deposit from LBU to Carl's account. That meant Carl was the first to try out the scam, at least based on the evidence I had.

Then I went back over all of the emails between Carl and Rita. There were only about a dozen, and the first eight related only to invoices and payments. Buried at the end of the ninth, though, Carl had written, "See you Saturday."

I went back to the receipts and cross-referenced the date, discovering that the Saturday in question was one that matched a receipt from the Newtown Arms.

That was good enough evidence for me.

I was ready to quit but I thought I'd better review the

last couple of emails again. The last one, dated a few days before Carl's death, was an eye-opener. "I can't keep doing this," he wrote. "If we get caught, with my record they'll send me right to prison. It's not worth the risk."

Rita hadn't answered him. But that gave Rita a powerful motive – if the goose refused to continue laying golden eggs, it was dangerous to let him keep squawking around her.

As an English professor, I understood I was mixing up genders. But the situation was the same. Add in the fact that in the past Carl had ratted out his collaborator, Big Diehl, and if I were Rita I'd be worried that Carl's new-found conscience could lead to big trouble.

Did Rita know anything about motorcycles, though? Maybe she didn't need to. She knew a lot of the other Angels, and she could ask one of them for information – or even convince one of them to meddle with Carl's bike in exchange for taking over his part in the false invoice scam. I even considered Travis at Pennsy Choppers, but I hadn't found any connection between him and Rita.

I sent Hunter an email with all the information I'd discovered on Rita. But I knew that he ran a one-man law firm with limited resources, and if I wanted to be sure Rita was the person who'd killed Carl, I had to meet her myself to get a feel for her. How could I do that? I didn't think I could go through Peggy, because she was pretty pissed at her sister.

I went online to the Liberty Bell University website and found a course on introduction to computer forensics. That was the kind of course I'd been considering, so I had a real reason to learn more about it, and LBU. I clicked on a link that said, "How can I pay for my courses," and was led to the financial aid page, with instructions on how to fill out my FAFSA, and the kind of aid programs students might quality for.

At the bottom of the page was a link that read, "Want to meet with one of our advisors? Click here!"

I did, and I came to a page featuring a calendar and instructions on how to make an appointment. I could choose "any advisor" or I could select one from a list.

Rita Corcoran's name was right there, and I clicked the link to set up an appointment with her. Her next available one was the next day, Wednesday, at three o'clock. The college was housed in a glassy high-rise in Langhorne, near the Oxford Valley Mall, and If I left Friar Lake at two, I could make it down there easily. I didn't think there was any danger she'd remember me, or my name, from one chance encounter twenty-five years before.

A note at the bottom of the web page said that service

animals were welcome at Liberty Bell University, and I looked over at Rochester. "What do you think, boy? Can you pretend to be a service dog?"

The year before at Halloween, I'd found a halter and vest in Rochester's size that read "Service Dog" on the side. I'd added "Dis" to the word service, so it read "Disservice dog" and considered the vest his costume.

I had read a lot online about people who pretended that various pets were service animals in order to take them on planes without paying. They claimed that their dogs, cats, even pot-bellied pigs eased their nerves when flying. One woman had even tried to take a peacock on a flight from New York to Miami as her service animal.

She'd been denied, of course. But that had raised a hue and cry about service animals on planes, leading many of the airlines to crack down.

I wasn't trying to get Rochester on a plane without buying him a ticket, and I did want to give him a chance to sniff Rita Corcoran and see what he thought of her. Nobody was going to arrest me for pretending he was my service dog, and I could say that he helped me with feelings of anxiety connected with going out in public. That would tie into my reason why I wanted to take online courses, and eventually get myself into a career I could do from home.

Lili returned a short while later, with a pair of new bathing suits, and she tried them on for me. The first was a form-fitting one-piece, with a scooped neck that dipped down into the curve of her breasts, and looked very sexy. The large blue and black lines were slimming – but of course I refrained from pointing that out.

The second looked almost more like lingerie than a bathing suit, with spaghetti straps over a rounded top and a flirty skirt with white waves against the black fabric. "I love them both," I said. "But then, I've always said you had good taste."

"I was reluctant to buy this one," she said, of the one with the tiny straps that she still wore. "But Tamsen convinced me."

"What kind of suit did she get?"

"She's more adventurous than I am, and skinnier, too. She bought a bright blue bikini and then another that looks kind of like this one, but in white."

"Rick's going to have to push his eyes back in his head," I said.

She slid down the straps of the bathing suit. "And you?" she asked.

"I love you no matter what you wear," I said. "Even if you're not wearing anything."

And that led where I wanted it to go. I pushed aside all thoughts of Peggy Landsea and her problems, and let myself live in the moment with Lili.

Rochester even obliged by slumping down on the floor in the bedroom doorway, as if he was protecting us while we were vulnerable.

# 22 – Disservice

Before I left for work the next morning, I dug out the service vest I'd converted into a Halloween costume and ripped off the extra "dis" from the word "disservice." I tossed it into the back of the car.

When I got to Friar Lake, I checked my personal email and found a message from Dee Gamay, the adjunct I'd emailed about working at Liberty Bell U.

"The place is a cluster-fuck," she wrote back. "If you can teach anywhere else instead, go for it. The administration is a bunch of money-grubbers who complain if you fail a student, even if they don't do the work."

Dee was clearly still as outspoken as she was when I knew her, which was good for my purposes. If LBU was really more concerned with taking students' money than educating them, then that kind of climate would make it easier for Rita to operate her Pell grant scam.

"You wouldn't believe the kind of emails that come out of that place, too," Dee continued. "It's as if the whole administration needs remedial writing skills because even the vice presidents make errors with comma splices and run-on sentences, and everyone seems to think that you should Capitalize Random Words."

I laughed, but at the same time I was sad. What was the use of pressing Eastern students to write properly if they got into a work world where that didn't matter?

Dee's final rant was about the use of the reply all button in emails. "It's bad enough to get a poorly written message the first time, but then it pops back into your in-box ten more times from people who keep including it. I have learned a lot about the kind of scams students put through from reading messages that aren't intended for me, though."

I thanked her for the advice and said I'd certainly push Liberty Bell U to the bottom of my search list. Then I sat back. The for-profit college seemed to embody all the worst things I'd read about such places—a focus on money and not on student success. A very welcoming environment for scams like the ones Rita appeared to be running.

I did some work and finished another one of the online courses the administration had prescribed for me, and after a quick lunch it was time to leave for my appointment with Rita Corcoran. Rochester was surprised when we left Friar Lake so early. But he enjoyed sticking his big head out the window and sniffing the afternoon scents, first on River Road and then on I-95.

Liberty Bell University didn't have a campus, just a couple of floors in a high-rise across the street from the

Sesame Place theme park. Convenient if Big Bird or Ernie needed some continuing education, I guessed.

I parked in the lot, but before we got out I fitted the vest onto Rochester and attached the harness. "Best behavior now, boy," I said to him, as I checked the fit. "You're going undercover as a service dog so you've got to play the part."

He gave me a big doggy grin and licked my face, and I laughed.

I let Rochester pee, then led him up to the front door. He wasn't happy with the short leash attached to the harness—he was accustomed to being a free-range dog, only limited by the six-foot-length of our ordinary leash.

"Heel," I said to him, tugging him beside me. He looked up at me.

"Don't give me that. You know what heel means." I leaned down and whispered in his ear. "Remember, you're under cover as a service dog."

Then I stood up again and pressed the automatic button for the sliding door into the lobby. A security guard sat behind a half-round desk, but she was more interested in her cell phone than in us, so I walked over to the display on the wall and found that the financial aid office was in suite 300.

Rochester behaved pretty well, sticking close to me as we rode in the elevator, though he might have been nervous about the unfamiliar surroundings. Either way he was playing the part of a service dog pretty well.

I pushed open the door to suite 300 and walked up to the reception desk. "I have an appointment with Ms. Corcoran at three," I said. "Steve Levitan."

She typed my name into her system and told me to have a seat. Either she didn't notice Rochester or she was accustomed to service animals accompanying their humans.

A few minutes later, a younger version of Peggy opened a door and called my name. At first glance she was far prettier than Peggy, though up close I could see she'd achieved that look with lots of makeup, and the smooth skin of her forehead and cheeks implied she'd had some work done as well.

"Are you a veteran?" she asked me. "I see you have a service dog."

"No, I have some social anxiety," I said. "Rochester helps me get over that in unfamiliar situations."

That wasn't far from the truth. "Well, service dogs are welcome on the Liberty Bell campus," she said.

Rita led the two of us down the hall to her office. "Why are you interested in Liberty Bell University?" she asked, as she sat down behind a generic office desk. Piles of folders on either side of her made a kind of a wall between us.

I explained that I was interested in computer forensics. "I have a job now, but I'm looking toward the future." I leaned in a bit, conspiratorially. "I also have a felony conviction on my record. Is that going to be a problem here?"

"How long ago?"

I gave her the timetable.

"No, it sounds like it won't be a problem," she said. "If you were still in prison, or if you served time for a drug-related offense, you'd be excluded from certain Federal programs like the Pell grants. But a computer offense doesn't matter for financial aid purposes."

She turned to her computer screen and started typing, then asked, "What was your gross taxable income last year? That's the first step in determining if you're eligible for a grant. Otherwise we'll have to look at loan programs."

I'd done some reviewing myself. I knew that most students who qualified for Pell Grants, the ones that Carl and the other Angels had been abusing, had family incomes of under $20,000. So I took a page from Rita's book and said that I'd made about nineteen grand the year before.

She smiled. "Good, that should make you eligible for a Pell Grant." She talked for a couple of minutes about what that meant, how much money I could get and so on.

I was more interested in her body language than in her

words. She seemed pretty open, like everything she was saying was the truth. Rochester was getting bored, though, so I thought I'd better move on. "My work hours can get kind of crazy," I said. "What happens if I start the class and can't finish it?"

"Then you'd fail," she said. "But as long as you do some work and try to pass the class, we won't hold it against you." She wagged a finger at me. "But the government is pretty strict about students who register for classes just to get the Pell Grant money and then never show up."

"You can do that?" I asked.

"You'd be surprised at how many people try that. It's part of my job to keep on top of that kind of behavior. Faculty members have to file reports with my office about students who don't show up for class, or, if they're registered in an online course, don't log in and do any work."

Interesting. If Rita was the one who collected that data, she could manipulate it.

We wrapped things up a few minutes later. I promised to go online and fill out the FAFSA, and she offered to help me if I ran into any problems. Then Rochester and I left.

We were in the elevator before I realized he had something in his mouth. I tugged it out and found it was a business card. Rochester had partly chewed off the name, but the rest of the card was intact, including a seal from the Office of Inspector General of the U.S. Department of Education.

# 23 – Her Own Sister

I was surprised that Lili wasn't home when I got there, because the summer term was so slow and she often slipped out an hour or two early. I fed and walked Rochester, and then got to work on a salad for our dinner, with grilled chicken strips over romaine lettuce, cherry tomatoes, green pepper strips and dried cranberries. I had just popped a loaf of frozen garlic bread in the oven when she came in.

"You're home late," I said. "Problems at the office?"

She shook her head. "No, everything's so quiet I left early and went walking around Leighville taking pictures. The town and the campus are so different during the summer. It has a kind of uninhabited look that intrigues me."

We talked about that, how Stewart's Crossing was a year-round kind of town, though it did have a lazier sense during the summer, with kids out of school and lots of families taking vacations.

"And yet, there's something dark underneath all the charm," I said. "People struggling to make payments on mega-mansions. Kids doing drugs."

"But that's everywhere. Look at your friend Peggy. She's had a tough life and keeps getting knocked down but she gets up again. I know how she feels, losing marriage after marriage." She looked up at me. "Think you're going to wrap everything up by the time we leave for the shore?"

"I think so. I have a couple of threads to chase down and then I'll present everything to Hunter. It's up to him what he does with it."

"And you're okay with that? With not solving the case? You've been pretty obsessed with that kind of thing in the past."

"I already think I know who's responsible. Peggy's sister, Rita. She was having an affair with Carl Landsea and also working with him on a couple of scams through her office."

I explained what I'd figured out so far. "I've already sent most of the information to Hunter. He can show it to the district attorney, and if I did my work right the DA will go after Rita. I get to solve the case without any of the confrontation or danger."

"That's a good thing," Lili said.

While Lili took care of the dishes, I wanted to follow up one of those loose threads I'd mentioned to her. I looked up the Office of the Inspector General online. It was tasked with investigating fraud, waste, abuse, mismanagement, or violations of laws and regulations involving Education Department funds or programs.

Did that include going after Pell scammers? Probably. But did it mean that the agency was actively investigating Liberty Bell University? This might have been a routine visit.

I could not find information on any open investigations, but after doing some digging I discovered that Liberty Bell U had already been cited several times for sloppy record-keeping, and had to pay some significant fines. That might mean Rita's bosses were looking into what she was doing, to stem the outflow of money back to the government, and that would put her whole operation at risk.

After I shut down the laptop I helped Lili go through her checklist of stuff to take with us to the shore on Sunday morning. I still needed to pick up some extra treats for Rochester and Rascal, and I promised to do that the next day on my way home from work.

Thursday morning I dropped Rochester at Friar Lake with Joey once again, and drove into Leighville for our in-person interviews with the final five candidates for the student life position.

I was glad that I got there early and was able to stop Dave Moretti from the financial aid office. "Can I ask you a question?"

"Sure."

I showed him the half-gnawed card. "This agency,

would they only show up on a campus if there was a suspicion of fraud? Or do they make routine visits, too?"

"Where'd you get this?"

"I had an appointment with someone at Liberty Bell University, and my dog got hold of this business card. I was curious about it."

He looked like he'd smelled something nasty. "Liberty Bell University is one of the most notorious of the for-profit colleges," he said. "Rife with scams and violations. I'm not surprised someone from the OIG was there."

We walked into the conference room together. "To answer your original question, I've never had a routine visit from the OIG, and I've never heard of anyone else who's had one. If this inspector was at Liberty Bell, then there's an open investigation."

I was fidgety through the interviews. Maybe Carl's death wasn't a case of killing the goose that laid the golden egg, but tying up loose ends. His last email to Rita had indicated that he wanted to get out, because he was afraid of going back to prison. If there was an active investigation, then he might have been tempted to rat out Rita in exchange for immunity, as he'd done with Big Diehl.

We finished all five interviews, and then met to prioritize our choices. I was pleased with the two candidates we recommended – both had significant experience working with high-achieving students like the ones at Eastern, and both were young and enthusiastic and not likely to burn out too quickly.

On my way back to Friar Lake I stopped at a hoagie shop in Leighville and picked up a roast beef sandwich with extra meat, which I shared with Rochester as an apology for abandoning him for most of the day.

When I finished eating, I called Hunter Thirkell and asked if I could stop by his office on my way home from work. "I want to go over that stuff I emailed you."

"I've been in court the last couple of days so I haven't had a chance to look through what you sent me. It's all legal, right? Stuff I can show to the DA?"

"Absolutely," I said, and out of habit I crossed my fingers. After I hung up, I started to put everything in order and make sure that indeed, I'd come by all the information legitimately. I printed out the emails between Rita and Carl, highlighting the last one where he wanted to stop working with her because he was afraid that if caught he'd be sent back to prison.

I added copies of the bank records, showing Carl's two types of income from Liberty Bell University and the way each deposit was matched with a transfer to Rita.

Rita had a motive to kill Carl – to keep him from ratting her out. If she went out with Carl, she'd have had the opportunity to fiddle with his bike.

The means was trickier, but I was going under the assumption that Rita worked with other bikers on the financial aid scam, and that she might have gotten one of them to show her the brakes on his bike, maybe even explain how they could be fiddled with. Or gotten one of the other scammers to meddle with Carl's brakes for her.

All in all, it was a convincing case that Peggy's sister should be considered a viable suspect in Carl's death, and that by presenting that information to the prosecutor, Hunter could kick off further investigation and maybe even get the charges against Peggy dropped.

Rochester and I walked into Hunter's office a few minutes after four and I handed him the folder of paperwork. I sat in the chair across from him, with Rochester on his haunches beside me. I scratched behind his ears as Hunter flipped through the paperwork.

"Her own sister," he said finally. "Jesus, what's the world coming to?"

"I know Rita was jealous of Peggy when they were kids, that Rita thought Peggy was too full of herself because she wanted to go to college. I doubt that's enough of a motive to ruin her sister's life now, but Peggy brought Carl into Rita's orbit, and I think he might have been the one to bring her those Social Security numbers. The fact that she was screwing her sister's husband probably didn't matter that much to her."

"And killing her brother-in-law?"

"He'd become a liability to Rita. So he had to go."

"This is good work, Steve. You ever think of becoming an investigator? I know a lot of attorneys who could use someone with some digital skills."

"Right now I'm set at Friar Lake," I said. "I'm considering taking some computer forensics courses, though. Try to channel my impulses into legitimate avenues, and give myself some credentials for the future."

"Can I call you again if I need some help? When a case isn't pro bono and I can pay you?"

"You can call, sure. Can't guarantee I'll be able to help you." I leaned forward. "What happens next?"

"Next? I meet with the prosecutor and give her this information. Then she decides how she's going to move forward with Peggy."

"And Rita?"

"That's up to the prosecutor. This is solid information, but of course she'll have to replicate it herself with her own investigators. And then she'll decide if she wants to press charges against Rita."

# 24 – Love and Hate

As I drove home, I felt bad for Peggy. Blood was supposed to be thicker than water. It was too bad that her worst enemy was turning out to be someone who should have had her back. Though as an only child, I knew I had an idealized version of what having a sibling would be like.

I called Peggy and asked if I could stop by her house on my way home. "You have more news?" she asked.

"I do. But I want to talk it over with you."

I got to her house a half hour later, and I saw the curiosity on Peggy's face as she let us in. "What's so important that you had to tell me face to face?"

We sat across from each other once again, Peggy on the sofa with Rochester beside her, and me in the recliner. Piece by piece, I went through the evidence that I'd passed on to Hunter.

When I finished, her mouth was open in horror. "You think Rita killed Carl?" she asked, and there was a plaintiveness in her voice that tugged at my heart strings.

"There's a lot of evidence that points her way," I said. "But remember, the police had a lot of evidence that implicated you, too. It's not up to either of us to make the final determination."

"Saturday afternoon should be interesting then," she said. "My sister Catherine, she's the touchy-feely one, wants the four of us to get together at RJ's house for lunch. Fortunately it's within the general area where I can go without getting permission from the judge."

"I don't think that's a good idea, Peggy," I said. "If I'm right, Rita killed Carl and she could be dangerous."

"I know how to deal with my sisters," Peggy said. "And if it comes down to that, I think Catherine and Anne will take my side against RJ. It's the first time Catherine has reached out to me, and I miss her and Anne. I feel like I have to go along with this."

She laughed bitterly. "Though I don't see why RJ is willing to agree to host us all if what you're saying is true."

"Take care of yourself, Peggy," I said. "Don't tell Rita anything that you and I have talked about, because if she's guilty you don't want her to come after you."

"I'm hoping it won't come to that," Peggy said. "Catherine says it'll be the four of us sitting around talking about the past." She looked wistful. "The good stuff, at least. Us getting out of Trenton, our mom happier."

I hoped that would be the case.

On my way home, I passed one of the big pet stores, and that reminded me that I'd promised to pick up some treats to take down the shore with us.

I took Rochester into the store with me, and as usual, the clerks all fawned over him—how beautiful he was, how well-behaved. I didn't mention he was also a crime-solving canine.

I loaded up a cart with rubber chews, bones stuffed with peanut butter, and more dental treats. I had to put the bag in the back to keep Rochester from nosing through it.

Friday morning I had to deal with a flurry of emails about the search committee, and make sure that I'd handled everything I had to before we left for our vacation. I met with Joey, and he and Rochester and I walked around the property and talked about the few things that might come up while I was away.

"I'll check my email at least once a day, but if something urgent comes up, feel free to call or text me."

"It's the summer. Nothing is going to be urgent," Joey said.

I kept hoping that Hunter would call me with the results of his conversation with the prosecutor, but maybe he hadn't been able to see her yet. Or maybe he'd figured I was done and now out of the loop.

Saturday morning Lili began checking items off on her to-do list, organizing piles of clothes on the dining room table, putting out the dog food and treats and so on. Rochester sensed something was going on and he kept getting underfoot. One of my jobs was to make sure that all our digital devices were charged, and that we had all the necessary cables.

Yeah, we'd promised to put those devices aside for a while and focus on being together, but Lili wanted to be able to take a lot of pictures and transfer them to her laptop. We both had to be able to check our emails, and maybe pull up a movie or two on the iPad.

It was early afternoon when Peggy called. "Steve?" she asked, and her voice sounded strangled. "I'm really frightened."

"What's the matter? "

"I'm at RJ's house, and she's on a rampage, ranting about problems and her work that somehow are my fault. Catherine and Anne are trying to stop her but she's not listening. I'm frightened."

"Walk away," I said. "You don't need to be in a toxic environment."

"I'm afraid if I do RJ will get even madder at me and go back to the police. She admitted that she's the one who told them that Carl was abusing me, even though it wasn't true. I don't know what else she could lie about."

"Why don't I come over there?" I said. "Sometimes having a third party there can defuse the anger."

"Could you? I hate to ask but I don't know what to do."

"Give me a half hour."

Lili looked up from her work at the dining room table. "You're not running out on me while I'm trying to organize everything, are you?"

"I won't be long. And I promise to do whatever you need when I get back."

"Fine. Go. But this is the end. Tomorrow morning we head for the shore and we're going to be on vacation from everything."

"I understand. And I'm with you one hundred percent." I kissed her cheek and hooked up Rochester's leash.

With him on the seat beside me, we retraced our steps to Rita Corcoran's house in Newtown. There were a couple of cars in the driveway and along the street, and I recognized Peggy's battered Nissan.

Once again I noticed how impressive Rita's house was, with perfectly manicured hedges and a group of pink roses in full bloom. What a contrast to the dump where Peggy lived.

As Rochester and I got out of the car, I heard the sound of an argument coming from the back yard, raised female voices. "You've always thought you were better than the rest of us," one voice said. "Because you went to college for a while. You were so ambitious that it made things harder for the rest of us who just wanted to get by. Teachers were always comparing me to you. Why can't you be as good a student as your sister? Shit, I hated that."

"I wanted to make things better for all of us," another voice said, one I recognized as Peggy's.

"Look around you, babe. I don't need you to do shit for me," Rita said.

"Please don't argue," a third voice said. "Can't we all get along, for once?"

"Shut up, Catherine," Rita said.

Then it sounded like all four sisters were talking at once and I couldn't make out what they were saying, until I heard Rita's voice rise above the din. "You'll see what happens to girls who try to be better than everybody else, Peggy. The cops are going to put you away for Carl's murder."

"But I didn't kill him," Peggy protested.

"I know that, babe. Believe me, I know that better than anybody. But it's still very sweet to see you hang for it."

"What are you saying, Rita?" Peggy demanded. "Do you know who killed Carl?"

"See what it's like, when you don't have all the

answers, college girl?" Rita said.

The voice I'd identified as Catherine's rose. "If you know who killed Peggy's husband then you're honor bound to tell the police. It's what sisters do for each other."

"I'll tell you what I did for Peggy. I used that asshole husband of hers as the dummy who took all the risks when I came up with the money-making schemes."

"Come on, RJ. You're not that smart," Peggy said. "Aren't you the one who's always complaining about me and my couple of years in college? Doesn't that make you too dumb to figure out any kind of scheme?"

I couldn't believe that Peggy was taunting Rita, when I'd told her specifically not to get her sister agitated and perhaps violent.

"How do you think I got this big house?" Rita said. "I came up with the schemes and got Carl and his buddies to put their names and on the line, and when he started to complain I took care of him, and managed to get back at the college girl for all the shit she gave us all those years."

I stepped away from the gate and called Rick. "Peggy's sister RJ just confessed to her and their other two sisters that she killed Carl Landsea and why." I explained that I was at Rita Corcoran's house in Newtown. "Can you come out here?"

"Not my jurisdiction," Rick said. "Landsea was killed in Tullytown."

"Can you call a cop over there?" In the background I heard the yelling continue.

"I'll see what I can do. Don't get yourself in the middle of the trouble." Rick rang off and I slipped the phone back in my pocket and let Rochester tug me toward the gate.

I'd missed some of the conversation, but the next thing I heard was Peggy saying, "Bitch!" and the sound of bodies colliding.

Despite what Rick had told me I had to jump in. I unlatched the gate, and as I did I let go of Rochester's leash, and he rushed forward.

Peggy was on the ground wrestling with Rita. Two other women stood there watching them, telling them to stop, but Peggy and Rita continued to go at it, rolling around on the ground, scratching and punching each other in what looked like an episode from one of the Real Housewives shows.

Rochester jumped in, as if this was the most fun he'd seen anywhere. He got between the two women, licking Rita on the face. "Yuck! Get this dog off me!"

She grabbed a hunk of his fur and pulled, and Rochester yelped. That was all it took to get me in there, too. Nobody hurts my dog while I'm there.

"Get your hands of him, you lousy tramp." I pulled her by the hair and she turned to me.

"You're that guy who came in for financial aid advice. What the hell are you doing here?" she asked, as Peggy got away and scrambled to her feet.

"He's my friend," Peggy said. Rochester went over to her and she petted him. "And his dog's my friend, too."

In the distance I heard a police siren. The two other sisters clustered around Peggy, comforting her, while I faced off against Rita. "You're not as smart as you think you are," I said. "You admitted to killing Carl Landsea in front of four witnesses. You're the one who's going to jail, not Peggy."

"I didn't admit to anything," Rita said defiantly. Her blonde bouffant had come loose and she'd lost two buttons on her blouse. Fortunately she wasn't as well-endowed as Peggy was after her surgery so it didn't matter.

She looked over at Rochester, who was digging for something under the boxwood hedge. "Get your dog out of there!"

"Rochester, come to me," I said, and as he did, I noticed a gold chain dangling from his mouth.

"That's Carl's St. Christopher medal," Peggy said. "The only time he ever took it off was to have sex, because he said he didn't want the saint watching him. He told me he lost it just before he died. What's it doing here?"

"I told you, Carl and I had meetings. He was over here one day and, you know how it is."

"You knew he was my husband and you still slept with him," Peggy said. "You're lower than dog turds, RJ."

"He thought you were a hot number, swinging around on poles at that miserable club, but then he figured out you were lousy in bed so he gave up on you and went looking for a woman who could really satisfy him."

"Girls!" Catherine said impotently. The other sister, Anne, stood there with her arms crossed, as if she was totally over the drama caused by her oldest and youngest sisters.

A Newtown police cruiser pulled up and the poor cop was overwhelmed by all four of the sisters trying to talk at once. I stood in the background with Rochester until Rick arrived, followed soon after by a detective from the Tullytown police department.

It took a while to get everything organized. The detective took the sisters into the house one by one to take statements from them, while Rick, the Newtown cop and I waited outside.

Eventually it was my turn, and I repeated everything I had heard that day. "What brought you over here?" he asked, when I was finished.

"Peggy called me. She was frightened by the way her sister was behaving, and at the same time she didn't want to leave because she was worried Rita would go back to you guys and make up more stuff that would implicate her in Carl's death."

"Not exactly a happy family reunion," the detective said, and left it at that.

* * *

Lili, Rochester and I left the next morning in a caravan with Rick, Tamsen, Justin and Rascal and drove down the shore. As we approached, I loved the sense that the land was so flat, that the horizon ahead of us stretched off toward the coast of Portugal.

While we were in Wildwood Crest, I got an email from Hunter Thirkell, thanking me for my help and letting me know that the police had dropped all charges against Peggy once they had assembled all the evidence against Rita. He reiterated his offer to hire me as an investigator in the future.

Peggy called to thank me for all my help. "Did you see that article in the Courier-Times?" she asked. "The reporter who called me the Black Widow had to add an apology to me in his story."

"I'll have to check it out." I hesitated. "Don't be a stranger again, okay, Peggy? We'll have to have you over for dinner soon. I want you to meet Lili, because you guys have a lot in common."

"I'd like that, Steve. I don't have many friends anymore, so I need to keep the ones I have. Like Hunter. He's been really good to me, and with the notoriety of my case, he's starting to get more business, so he's going to hire me as his legal secretary."

"That's awesome, Peggy."

"And I might even go back to college part-time and finish my bachelor's. I only need about another year. Who knows, I might even end up going on to law school myself."

It was terrific to see the old Peggy coming through, returning to her earliest hopes and dreams.

I checked out the Courier-Time story after I hung up with Peggy. It wasn't as much of an apology as Peggy thought, more an exploration of the way the blame had shifted to Peggy's sister, with a hint of more revelations to come.

Rochester came over and nuzzled his head against my knee. I had long since come to trust his instincts when it came to people. He knew who was good and who wasn't. He'd liked Peggy Doyle from the start, and hadn't liked her sister Rita.

Over the next week, I taught Justin how to play gin rummy, and Lili took him out on a couple of photographic excursions. Rick and I hung out, drinking beer and talking about everything from our dogs to old classmates. Tamsen and Lili continued to bond, and Rochester and Rascal had a great time romping and then sleeping against each other.

There was a lot of love in that house, and I hoped that love like that would be out there for Peggy Landsea, too.


Thanks for reading! I'd love to stay in touch with you. Subscribe to one or more of my newsletters: **Gay Mystery and Romance** or **Golden Retriever Mysteries** and I promise I won't spam you!

Follow me at **Goodreads** to see what I'm reading, and my **author page** at Facebook where I post news and giveaways.

If you liked this book, please consider posting a brief review at your vendor, at Goodreads and in reader groups. Even a short review help other readers discover books they might like. Thanks!


Here is the series in order:

1. *In Dog We Trust*

2. *The Kingdom of Dog*

3. *Dog Helps Those*

4. *Dog Bless You*

# Acknowledgments

I would like to acknowledge the support of my colleagues at Broward College, and my fellow members of Mystery Writers of America, as well as the faculty of the creative writing department at Florida International University, where I received my MFA.

My cousin Scott Globus provided useful information on cameras. And I am always grateful to my husband Marc and our golden retrievers, Brody and Griffin, who continue to inspire me with their antics.

Printed in Great Britain
by Amazon

81337324R00161